THE ELVES AND THE BONDAGE DADDY

Grim Delights

JP SAYLE

A DADDY DOM, TWO NAUGHTY VIRGIN ELVES AND AN INTERFERING FATHER, WHAT COULD POSSIBLY GO WRONG?

Benidic and Gwil know their future is to be bonded to each other, but as much as they love each other there is something missing in their lives.

That is until Drake.

Drake is down on his luck. His shoe making business has closed and he must find another income. Then he gets an offer from the owner of the club he frequents to make BDSM bondage wear. But there's a problem, he needs assistance. Can the two men who break into his shop provide the answer? Or is trying to teach two naughty Elves what happens when you mess with a Daddy Dom just the start of his problems?

The Elves and the Bondage Daddy is a standalone mmm gay romance with delightful dark twists, enough steam to melt your panties and a HEA.

Trigger Warning: *Dubious Consent, BDSM, Daddy Kink.*

Every book is a voyage and without Guy, HL, Mandy, Julie, and Tina's support that journey might be a lot harder to navigate. Thank you for everything, much to love you all.

PROLOGUE

The king sat on the throne in front of me, a formidable scowl on his usually stunning face. It was a face that resembled my own. It should have done. He was my father after all. His face was twisted with a raw anger that caused the room to vibrate and my skin to hum unpleasantly. Gwilym, or Gwil to me, had been my best friend since birth and my boredom had yet again got us both into hot water. There was so little to do in the Elvedom that we had to make our own fun in order to keep us entertained.

"Why do I always have to repeat myself with you two? The last time you decided to have some fun, it took weeks to repair the damage to the palace, even with the use of collective magic."

The agitation in my father's voice forced me to keep a straight face. I did my best not to look over at Gwil, who stood next to me with his head bowed as Father berated us both again.

Why couldn't he understand that it was boring without making up games to play?

"Do you forget that as your father, I can read your thoughts, Benidic?" His silver brows merged into one straight line, his pale aqua eyes boring into mine. The strength of his magic made it impossible for me to move. "The games you play cause harm to others. You've become a thoughtless, spoiled brat and a nuisance to those who inhabit the palace." His gaze shifted to Gwil with a look of disappointment before moving back to me again. He sighed loudly.

The sound caused unease to unfurl in my stomach as he leaned back on his majestic throne. It glittered with the jewel colours of Elvedom. Our home was situated in a magical realm outside the earthly plane. A place that the earth dwellers had long since forgotten existed. The Elves created magic to protect the fabric of the earthly realm. The protector Elves worked day and night to ensure that the otherworld and other magical creatures had the magic needed to sustain life.

Those that dwelled in the magical realm never aged once they'd reached the age of maturity for Elves at three hundred earth years. I was still a long way off hitting maturity and those long eons stretched endlessly before me.

I eyed the jewelled throne that would one day be mine once Father decided I was ready, as his father had done, and his father before him, stretching back over the millennia. As the thought filled me with dread, I worked to shield my mind.

The Elvedom was filled with light and love. I, on the other hand, craved something more, something... a little darker. But with no experience beyond the realm, I had no idea what it was. So instead I created mayhem to fill the space inside me which felt empty and needy.

Father tapped a long, pale finger against his lips as they

pursed. The unease inside me increased as his eyes narrowed. "I think I need to teach you both a lesson. One that shows the other Elves that I'm not going soft when it comes to the pair of you." He shifted forward, his long flowing robes of gold shimmering in the light. "Magic is a gift, and as such it should be treasured and not used for mischief. With that in mind,"—he lifted his hands, light shining from both palms as orbs floated above him—"from now on, your hands will only be able to create magic that assists others with no gain for either of you. I banish you to the earthly realm to fend for yourselves until you can prove that you are worthy to return."

My heart thumped against my ribs as Gwilym cried out, but it was already too late. The air moved around us, speeding so fast that my long silver tresses blew around my face. I reached for Gwil, gripping his hand as the world around us became a blur before simply disappearing. The reassuring sensation of Gwil's palm against mine kept me from crying out as panic seized my chest.

The world finally came back into focus but there was only darkness. I blinked rapidly, trying to see something. What was this?

In the Elvedom there was no darkness, only light.

When all I could see was an inky blackness that offered nothing, no light, no hope, an incessant buzzing started in my ears. I lifted my hand in an attempt to create light, releasing a cry when nothing happened. My father's words rang inside my mind. "Your hands will only be able to create magic that assists others."

"Oh, to the heavens! What have we done, Benidic?" Gwil cried out, the sound echoing. I twisted towards him, holding onto his hand as a lifeline.

Seconds passed, the darkness receding a little as my

eyes began to adjust. I squeezed Gwil's hand harder. "We've messed up. Dear Elvedom, what are we to do? I know my father and he will not bring us back until he is satisfied that we have suffered." A shiver raced down my spine as I inhaled an odd smell. "What is that awful stench?" I said through gritted teeth, doing my best not to open my mouth.

"It... it smells like rotten food," Gwil offered, inching even closer to me.

His warm body pressed against the length of mine, the fragrant scent of lavender taking the edge off my panic. I wrapped my arms around him and inhaled his scent. The weight of his body against mine was familiar due to the fact that we'd often shared a bed together growing up. His father was the head of the Elvedom protectors which gave him a place of honour in the Elvedom. Most of my memories included Gwil. We were both aware of our fathers' hopes that once we'd matured, we would mate and bond, as was customary of our kind. I loved Gwil like no other, yet there was something missing. Neither of us had spoken about it though, me because of my inner craving and him... well, I didn't know why he hadn't said anything.

To distract myself from the shivers racing down my spine, I recalled my history lessons about Earth.

"Look down there. Is that light? Maybe we can find someone to help us," Gwil exclaimed, not sounding at all convinced that that might happen.

I looked towards the light to see movement... people. Excitement pulsed to life, my fear decreasing. *The stories about humans showed that they could be kind.* The thought giving me hope, I propelled Gwil towards where the people were. I popped my head out to look around, Gwil whimpering and clinging to me.

The street lights showed dark grey floors and buildings made out of concrete and brick. Humans walked on the other side of the street, their clothes so different from our flowing robes.

I glanced down, my eyes widening at the dark trousers and thick coat which had replaced my silk trousers and robe. It was only then that I registered that Gwil wore something similar to me. "It would appear Father has thought of everything," I said, the reality that we wouldn't be going home any time soon, sinking in.

"But what are we going to use as coin to buy the things we need?" Gwil fretted as he dug his hands into every pocket in the clothes he could find, coming up empty every time.

"We'll think of something. We have to." Tears clogged my throat as I tugged Gwil towards me. "We're going to be fine, you'll see. All we need to do is find someone to help with our magic and we'll be home in no time." I added, putting as much conviction into my voice as I could, Gwil's eyes sheening with tears. "You'll see, I promise."

I just prayed to the Elves of the otherworld that I could keep my promise.

CHAPTER ONE

Drake

The sounds coming from overhead as I walked from the shop into the other half of the building which was my home, made my stomach drop. The writing had been on the wall for weeks, but I'd foolishly thought that Sonny and I could weather the storm.

I'd just had to close down my handmade leather shoe business due to the economic downturn. When I'd discussed the possibility with Sonny weeks earlier, I'd noticed how distant he'd become. The gravy train he'd been riding was about to come to an abrupt halt, and when I'd left him that morning to go down to the shop, a sense of unease had settled in the pit of my stomach.

I tilted my head to listen to the sound of wardrobe doors opening and closing. I sighed with resignation as I walked down the hallway and up the stairs. Stepping into the bedroom, I eyed the bed before turning my attention to Sonny, who didn't acknowledge my presence. "Why are you packing?"

His blond head didn't lift once. "I'm leaving."

"What do you mean you're leaving?" I stood perfectly still, for fear of doing something I'd regret as Sonny continued to shove clothes, clothes *I'd* bought, into his suitcase—one of three on the bed.

Sonny had been my boy and my sub for the last two years, and although deep down I'd known that this was coming it still came as a shock. Recently, I'd only just been keeping my head above water enough to pay the bills.

I'd hoped that Sonny would go out and get a job to help out, but that had appeared to be a step too far. The selfish fucker was showing his true colours now, and although I hadn't been completely blind to his nature, I'd stupidly thought that he'd want to help me now when I needed it the most.

I stepped back from the bed, hands clenching as I eyed Sonny, anger simmering inside me. "You do know that I paid for all those things you're packing?" I rasped past my dry throat.

His hair shifted around his pretty face as he finally turned to face me. He gave a nonchalant shrug. "And your point is? You bought them for me. It's not like they'd fit anyone else. These are my reward for staying and putting up with you. You never really wanted me, not just me anyway. You were always looking for a third. That shows that you'll never be satisfied with me. I'm just cutting the ties now before feelings get involved." The words sliced at my heart, cutting it to ribbons.

I reached out to hold on to the wooden bedpost, my legs unsteady. I'd purchased the bed with plans to have both a permanent sub *and* a boy. Sonny had put paid to the latter, his jealous nature meaning that whenever I bought a third into our bed, he'd do his best to piss the boy off so they'd leave. I'd stopped trying after the third attempt and focused all my attention on him. Now he was using the need I'd never hidden as a weapon against me. Why had I ever thought I had feelings for this ungrateful shit?

I hardened my heart against the emotions rolling through me and breathed through the pain. Masking my expression, I nodded. "You're right, it must have been hard for you to sponge off me for two years. To have me pay for everything your heart desired while you lazed about in *my* home."

I gestured towards the third wardrobe, which I'd purchased for the additional clothes he'd felt he needed, a wardrobe that was still full. "They can stay. I think you've packed all that you're going to take from my home." I glanced at the suitcase and then back to him. "I'll help you to the door."

Saying nothing more, I slammed the lid down on the two closest suitcases, ignoring Sonny's huffs as I did so. When I'd zipped up both cases, I tugged them off the bed, my arms straining under the weight. "After you," I ground out through my clenched jaw.

His face turned a deep shade of red as he grabbed the remaining suitcase and staggered to the door with it. "You're a cunt," he muttered under his breath.

Seething, I nevertheless held my tongue as I followed him down the stairs to the front door.

At the bottom of the stairs, he reached for the bunch of keys that held my house key and the car key—a car I'd bought so he could have use of it to visit friends. I dropped the cases and they thudded on the wooden floor as I placed my hand over his. "I don't think so. The car is in my name and you won't need the house key."

His face scrunched up into a mutinous scowl. "You

never use it!" he shouted. His spittle hit my face but I didn't let go of his hand.

"That might be, but it belongs to me. I've paid for it. I bought it because the man, who I thought loved me and wanted to be a part of my life, said he needed it. I was mistaken. As you've no need for my love, then you'll have no need for the car either." I squeezed his hand hard, desire flaring to life in his eyes. I sighed in disgust at the look I knew only too well. Him being a pain slut was what had attracted me to him in the first place.

That look though, had no effect on me now, not when all I felt was anger. "That won't work anymore." I snatched the keys from his hand without giving him time to respond.

I wasn't even sure why I was surprised that he felt he had the right to take the car, because while I'd been deluding myself that he loved me, he'd walked right over me.

I was a foolish old fucker.

He glowered at me as I stepped back. "Then order me an Uber."

Refusing to have an argument when all I wanted was for him to leave so I could lick my wounds in private, I dug my phone out of my back pocket and ordered a car to pick him up, resigned to paying for that too. The bitching and moaning that followed as we waited for it to arrive caused my head to pound and my eyes to ache.

By the time the car had pulled away from the curb, all I wanted to do was find a dark room and close my eyes, to shut out the world that was doing its best to kick my arse. I headed up to the bedroom pausing in the doorway to survey the messy room. The scent of Sonny's expensive aftershave lingered, my nose burning as I struggled to swallow.

It's over. It's in the past, move on.

How can it be in the past when he's only just left?

Unable to argue with the logic, I walked over to the bed to lie down. I laid my forearm over my face as I closed my eyes, hoping that when I opened them again things would seem brighter.

CHAPTER TWO

Gwil

My love for Benidic had been my undoing on many occasions, but this beat all the others hands down. My beloved had always had an adventurous heart. It had drawn me to him like a butterfly to a flower. Right now though, with hunger pains growing in my stomach and the smell of my own stale body, I couldn't find the love I normally felt for the adventures he took me on.

Three days of tramping the streets had had me swearing to never give in to Benidic again. *Dream on, you know the moment he flutters his incredibly long, silver lashes at you, that you'll cave like you do every time.*

I gave a mournful sigh, shifting my bottom on the hard, wooden bench that I'd been sat on for the last hour while waiting for Benidic to return. We'd found some humans who weren't trying to sell us something, or take money we didn't have to answer our questions and we'd discovered that we were in a place called London. We'd also figured out how the element of time worked in this world. It seemed the day was governed by hours which turned into days and then weeks and so on. If I wasn't so scared, I'd have found the learning fun. The history we'd been taught at home had focused on the legends and lore of the human world, which had been about as useful as our empty pockets when it came to needing to blend in.

My stomach snarled with hunger, a sob rising in my throat. I quickly swallowed it and swiped at my cheeks as I felt the wetness against my skin. "Tears show weakness," I recited over and over, hoping that it would help.

"Are you okay? You're talking to yourself, you know that right?" said a deep voice that held authority, but also concern.

I lifted my head to look in the direction the voice had come from. My breath caught in the back of my throat as my gaze travelled up long, muscular legs. The man stood well over six feet, his body encased in similar dark clothes to those I wore. His upper body was massive and his broad chest seemed to stretch for miles. Sensations hummed to life inside me, sensations that were nothing like the ones Benidic stirred in me.

What is happening to me?

I stiffened.

He was like no one I had ever met before. Most of the elvish men were slim-built and none stood this tall, not that I could recall anyway. I licked my lips as I met his hooded gaze.

His eyes were the colour of a stormy sea, somewhere between green and dark grey. And his hair was a similar colour to mine—inky black. Only his was threaded with silver and showed his human years. His full lips pulled up into a warm smile and my stomach fluttered alarmingly, heat spreading through my body. The tiny licks of pleasure that followed made me swallow a moan.

What is wrong with me? Am I coming down with some human illness?

"Gwil!" Before I could pull myself together, I heard my name shouted. I sagged in relief, shifting to the side to peer around the guy as Benidic came running across the park. He'd left me to go and see if he could find us some food.

His long hair shone in the sunlight as it swung around his shoulders like a silver cape. His eyes revealed his concern, so I stood and stepped around the man, doing my best to act like a human.

Whatever Benidic's father had done when he'd sent us here, he'd masked some of our more obvious differences. However, the grace and fluidity with which we moved was not something we'd witnessed in human males. Neither was our almost translucent skin which caused some to stare at us. We'd done our best to try and blend in, and I'd even suggested that maybe we should cut our hair. Mine, though raven black, was equally as long as Benidic's and reached my lower back. It didn't seem to be something common in the human men we'd seen so far.

Benidic had thrown a fit at the very idea of me cutting off my hair. His tendency to lie next to me and bury his face in it when he needed comfort had prevented me from mentioning it again.

He came straight over to me and wrapped his arm around my waist, his show of possession doing funny things to me as the man stared at us with an interest that set my pulse to racing.

"Can we help you?" Benidic asked, his voice shrill.

I glanced at him from beneath my eyelashes before looking at the man. My heart beat a little faster as the man stood taller, his face morphing into a mask of indifference. But I'd already caught the flicker of desire in the depths of his eyes. I clutched at Benidic as I chewed my lower lip between my teeth. Would Benidic do something stupid, like challenge the man?

Benidic had learnt all the skills of Elf fighting. He was good at it, but seemed to take great pleasure in letting others inflict pain on him. After sparring sessions, he'd refused to let me use my magic to heal him and remove the marks that covered him.

I shook off the memory, unsure why this man would make me think about such things.

"Your friend was talking to himself. I was concerned so I stopped to check if he was alright." The deep husky voice drew my attention as Benidic's body shuddered against mine, his breathing speeding up.

"I'm fine," I lied, unconvincingly if the man's expression was anything to go by.

He lifted his powerful shoulders before nodding. "If you're sure." His eyes narrowed on us both. "I'll leave you to it then." The man lifted his hand in a wave before spinning around and walking off down one of the many paths in the park.

"What were you playing at, Gwil? I told you not to talk to anyone when I'm not around to protect you." Benidic's voice sounded strained, but his gaze stayed on the tall figure disappearing into the distance. "That man wanted... us." He muttered it, almost as if it was an afterthought, his slim brows rising and the look on his face twisting my gut into knots.

"Whatever you're thinking, stop right now." But I got no further finding myself dragged along with him as he took off in the same direction the man had gone. I dug my heels into the ground. Or at least I tried to, but Benidic was wily, twisting his arm around my waist to pull me with him, my feet barely touching the ground. "What are you doing?" I hissed through clenched teeth.

"I'm trying to come up with a plan that allows us to help a human and get home. There was something about him that spoke to me. I think he needs help... so we're going to follow him," he stated in a low tone, not sounding out of breath even though he was practically carrying me.

The show of strength awakened the yearning that was never too far away now that we were on Earth, which made it hard to think. In the few seconds it took to register what he'd said, he'd already sped up.

"What... no... that man... there is something about him." I shuddered, unable to explain how conflicted I felt about it all. I bit my lip, my jaw clenching in an effort to stop any silly words from pouring out. I longed to express the new feelings I had for Benidic, but I'd acknowledged long ago that he needed more than I could offer him, despite the expectation that we would mate. Maybe this man could help?

Don't be silly, how can he help?

A ripple of awareness sparked deep in my chest that I didn't want to explore further, so I let Benidic lead as I always did, hoping that this time it would all end differently.

You do know Benidic has trouble embedded in his magical soul, don't you?

CHAPTER THREE

Drake

Shoving my hands into my pockets, I took several deep breaths, hoping that the scent of freshly cut grass would ease the tension in my body. It continued to linger though as I fought the urge to look back at the two men I'd found so intriguing. Men that spoke to both sides of me in a way I'd never encountered before. The way they'd touched each other had set fire to the spark of dark desire in me. One that I'd kept hidden, buried deep in the darkest part of my heart.

When I'd entered the world of BDSM some twenty years earlier, I'd discovered a darkness inside me that, once awoken, I'd struggled to find a way to balance. That was why I'd always known I needed both a sub and a boy. The first to let me fly into the darkness and the second to keep me tethered to the light. The years had passed and I'd failed to find a pair who fit me. This failure had had me hiding my true nature. I'd thought that I'd never find what my soul craved, believing I'd made peace with it. But after today, I was no longer so sure—all my want and desire resurfacing.

The sight of the scruffy young man on the bench, who

the other one had called Gwil, had called to me. Long raven hair flowed down his back and gleamed like onyx in sunlight. His thin shoulders, slumped as they were, had spoken of a sadness inside him. My Daddy side had hummed in recognition of what he was, the allure so strong that I'd been compelled to get closer.

I'd walked over to him, hearing him mutter something about tears showing weakness, and I'd wanted to... to do what?

I'd pushed what I'd wanted to do aside. The hurt Sonny had inflicted mere days ago was still too fresh a wound to ignore. Not that there'd been an opportunity to act on my impulses, not when in response to my simple question, he'd raised his head and I'd been left deaf, dumb and blind to everything for those few seconds except the violet eyes that met mine. They had to be contacts. No one had eyes that colour.

Then why did I feel like they were real?

I shook my head as the silver eyes of Gwil's friend swam in front of me. My body juddered at what those eyes had revealed. There'd been something exotic in their depths, a craving for... the dark.

Jeez, stop it with the psychoanalysis bullshit.

Those men are probably as vanilla as a plain sponge cake, so get over it.

I sighed, trying not to think about how much I'd like to strap blondie to my pillory and do all the things I suspected he wanted while the raven-haired beauty was tied to the bed, watching us with his strange eyes.

Fuck, stop!

The hard length of steel which had replaced my dick made it difficult to walk normally as I exited the park. I attempted to readjust it without any of the people swarming around noticing.

Ignoring the sounds that never stopped in the city, I walked for several minutes before I caught sight of my shop at the far end of the street. The dark, empty windows cooled my ardour immediately and reminded me why I'd gone out in the first place. After checking my abysmal bank balance, I'd been forced to ring my friends looking for a way to make enough income to keep me afloat until I'd decided what I was going to do with my business.

What business?

I swallowed a sigh, thinking back to the meeting I'd had with Richard that morning. He was the owner of the BDSM club I frequented. He'd heard on the grapevine that I was looking for work and had asked me to come down to the club to talk over an idea he had. What I hadn't expected was a request to make replacement furniture for the club.

It wasn't a secret that I had my own playroom at home, a playroom which contained specially handcrafted pieces of furniture I'd made. It was a side interest I'd had for many years. I'd always been creative so over the years I'd tried my hand at many things, picking up numerous skills along the way and finding an affinity for working with leather, wood and metal.

Leather had always been my first love to work with, my father encouraging me to take over his business when he'd retired ten years earlier. Having apprenticed for him for so many years, it was an easy decision to make to take over designing the handmade shoes. I'd been content when the business was thriving, but these days handmade shoes were an expense that many couldn't afford.

Richard's offer might solve my problem, but was it what I wanted to do?

Initially I'd laughed off his suggestion because I couldn't see how a hobby could turn into more. That was the reason for taking the detour through Regents Park, a way of giving myself time to turn the idea over in my mind and consider the skills I had. The idea had grown on me and for some reason, it had only increased when... *nope, don't go there.*

It took effort, but I retuned my thoughts to Richard, erasing two pairs of eyes from my memory banks. He'd walked me through it in the club explaining all the things he wanted replaced, as well as the new ideas he had to drum up more business. It had been enough to spark my interest.

With the shop in sight, I mentally went through my inventory of stock in the storeroom, as well as the tools in the large outbuilding I worked in. The problem was that some of what Richard required would mean I needed help, and with no way of paying anyone I didn't know how I'd manage on my own.

Distracted from my thoughts by voices around me, I stopped at the curb, waiting impatiently for the lights to change. I stood straighter as people crowded around me, putting my stern Dom face into place to get them to back off. People shifted away and I breathed a little easier.

I hated to be crowded.

A shiver slid down my spine as I scratched my neck while kinking my head from one side to the other. I glanced around cautiously, but saw nothing that would set off any alarm bells. Yet the feeling of unease wouldn't leave me alone.

I looked from side to side, pulling my hands out of my pockets in case I needed to defend myself, but I still saw nothing that could cause me this level of alarm. I'd lived in London for decades and I wasn't oblivious to those who could go from smiling at you one minute, to trying to stab you the next. I let out a relieved breath as the beeping noise indicated I could cross. Shifting over to the edge of the crowd, I made my way to the side street which led to the back entrance of my shop.

Once inside the door, I was driven to go over to the window which overlooked the main street. Peering out onto the busy pavement, I froze, my lungs seizing hold of the air I'd just inhaled. There, on the other side of the street, stood the two men I'd encountered in the park. A dark hunger unfurled like a rattlesnake getting ready to strike. I clutched at the empty shelf in front of the window, the need to go back outside, take hold of the two men and drag them into the shop with me growing.

Had they followed me? Why would they do that?

Had my instincts been right about them after all? *Or maybe they were just heading in this direction, you moron?*

Even as the thought registered, I shook it off. No, they'd followed me. I was sure of it. But why? That was the question I couldn't answer.

CHAPTER FOUR

Benidic

When I'd returned to find the man standing over Gwil, I'd not had time to register the instant pull in my groin until I'd wrapped my arm around Gwil. Then I'd had plenty of time to become aware of the power of the attraction. Something deep inside me had expanded. It was like the feel of magic, except it wasn't magic. It was a deep-seated, burning need. Right alongside it had been the urge to get down on my knees and submit to the man. It left me breathless and unsure of myself like never before.

As I'd practically lifted Gwil off his feet in order to keep the man in my sights, I'd recalled the strange lack of possessiveness I'd felt at the man's open appreciation of Gwil. In our realm, when other Elves had eyed Gwil with interest the same way the man had, I'd been desperate to fight to show them that he belonged to me. Yet this time, I'd had a moment of clarity, a moment of recognising how it could be with this man, and my heart and soul had trembled.

In all of the years that I'd spent loving Gwil, a part of me had always known he'd never be able to satisfy me the way I needed. I still wanted him to belong to me and I couldn't conceive of him not being my mate, ours souls bonded together when the time came. But that didn't stop the dark craving.

There was a light inside Gwil that couldn't be dimmed which made me want to take care of him, to meet his need to be told what to do. Something I'd happily do for the rest of my eternal life because my love for him was limitless, but that didn't stop the part of me that wanted... more.

"He'll never be enough to assuage the hunger for pain," the dark part whispered inside me.

My heart beat erratically against my ribs as the man we were following slowed, my body reacting to the dominance he naturally exuded. His powerful body fascinated me, my mouth watering at the thought of how I might worship him. Carnal thoughts that were usually hidden deep inside me rose, awakening my sexual spirit.

My mouth opened but no words came out as I clung tighter to Gwil

Had the bindings that controlled our sexual urges been removed in this realm? It took a minute to register the differences in my body: the magical restraints placed on us as fledgling elves that prevented us from losing control were gone. I panted through the excitement at what this could mean. *Oh, to the Elvedom! Sexual freedom.*

The warmth of the sun made the clothes I was wearing unbearable against my soft skin, sweat gathering on my brow. Wearing the same clothes for three days continuously had chafed my sensitive flesh that was so used to fine silks. The human clothes were stiff and rough. Sleeping in them in the homeless shelter we'd found on the second night hadn't helped matters either.

I shuddered at the thought of having to spend another

night on the soiled camp beds they'd offered to us. We'd helped with some of the basic chores, assisting with a touch of magic to make the food edible. Any thoughts that it might be enough to appease Father had died on the third night.

When Gwil had climbed in the small bed with me, the guy who ran the shelter had told us, in no uncertain terms, that it was forbidden to share beds. After that, Gwil had cried himself to sleep in the bed next to mine. It had broken my heart when he'd turned his back on me.

Ever since then, he'd become more distant. Despair had had me searching for food on my own today in the hopes of getting into Gwil's good graces once more. The sound of Gwil's stomach snarling had made me realise that I'd failed him yet again. With my mind full of concern, I'd followed a gut instinct which said not to let this man out of my sight, no matter how reluctant Gwil might be.

"Let him cross before we follow," I whispered into Gwil's ear. He balled his hand into a fist. "Please, we need to see where he's going. I swear that my soul is telling me that he's the one we need to help."

When Gwil sighed with resignation and sagged against me, I took it as agreement. The people surged forward and for a second, I lost sight of the man as he disappeared. I released the breath that had got caught in my chest as he appeared again as the crowd dispersed on the other side of the road. My relief was only fleeting though as he disappeared down a side street.

If I was reading the sign correctly, it was a dead end meaning he had to have gone into one of the buildings. I eyed the window of the closed shop, gazing up at the sign above it when the empty shelves didn't reveal what kind of shop it was. The sign said, *The Shoemaker*, but there was no evidence of any shoes. I squinted, trying to see farther into the shop, but the darkness revealed nothing except shadows.

I held on to Gwil as he started to squirm next to me, glancing at his distressed face as we moved out of the way of the next wave of people getting ready to cross the road.

"Can't you feel his eyes on you?" Gwil whimpered, his gaze moving from me to the shop.

I shifted back to stare at the windows. For a second, I thought I caught sight of a dark head peering out of one of the windows on the far side of the shop. But when I blinked, there was nothing there. I shook my head, trying to shake off the same feeling Gwil had just expressed. Could I feel his eyes on me? And if so, what did that mean?

PEERING INTO THE DARKNESS, I JERKED AS THE LIGHT coming from the window above the shop the man had gone into went out. The sound of my breathing filled my ears as I shifted from a crouched position. It took a moment for my legs to adjust to the sensation of blood flowing back through them after being folded for hours. Once they'd returned to normal, I crept silently to the end of the alleyway. I'd seen the alley after I'd led Gwil away from the shop window. I looked up and down the street, cursing under my breath.

There were still so many people walking around that I struggled to contain my frustration, my hands twitching uselessly at my sides. If I'd had my magic, I could have cloaked both Gwil and myself so that we couldn't be seen. *If you had your magic, you wouldn't be here!*

I stilled at the thought, especially when it dawned on me how much I wanted to follow where my soul was leading me. I glanced back at Gwil's slumped form as he slept on the ground, his face masked by the darkness of the alley. Regret filled me as I thought of all the suffering he'd endured for the last few days. I clutched my chest, hoping to ease the ache that seemed to increase with each passing day at the realisation that I couldn't fix what I'd done.

I glanced back at the dark window, struggling to come to terms with the part of me that wasn't in the least bit sorry. What if what I felt inside for this man was real and he'd released it from me?

Then you'll find your truth.

Will I?

On legs that trembled and with a mind in turmoil, I walked back over to Gwil to wake him.

I crouched next to Gwil, my knees cracking in protest as I whispered into his ear, "Come on sleepy head, wake up."

His eyelashes fluttered open and I exhaled quickly as a sleepy smile spread across his sexy face. The awakening of my sexual need tugged low in my belly as I lowered my mouth to brush my lips gently against his.

He hummed before wrapping his arms around my neck. My dick started to plump for the first time in my long life, again making me consider the breaking of the bindings that normally kept our desires in check. A groan rumbled in my throat as I opened my mouth to deepen the kiss. Sensations flooded through my body, awaking every nerve ending. They thrummed with energy and with life and I moaned, overwhelmed with the need for more.

Gwil's hot breath merged with mine as he opened for me and I got my first taste of him. It was intrinsically him, yet somehow more intoxicating. All thoughts disappeared as his tongue brushed tentatively against mine. The kiss, a first for both of us, went from one gentle caress to the next. I explored his mouth leisurely, learning what it felt like to kiss another. But then the whimpers he made were lost to the loud blare of a siren, pulling me from the sexual haze which had descended upon me.

I gasped as I released his lush mouth to meet his stunned expression. The love I knew he'd always felt shone from his trusting eyes. With the need to do more than just kiss lurking under the surface, I forced myself to stand. The dark and dirty alley was not the right place for what I had in mind. I looked back at the dark building, staring at Gwil as I offered him my trembling hand. "Let's go and meet our destiny." The words had formed somewhere deep inside me, coming out with utter conviction and causing Gwil's eyes to widen briefly before a look I'd come to understand settled on his face.

He took the hand I held out to him, rising fluidly with his gaze holding mine. "Then let it be so my... love."

CHAPTER FIVE

Drake

Punching the pillow for the umpteenth time, I buried my face in it. When I closed my eyes and all I could see were the two men from the park, I swore under my breath. They had haunted me all afternoon and evening. I'd watched through the window from out of the shadows as they'd disappeared up the street. It had taken several reminders of what had happened with Sonny to stop me from following them.

Let it go, for fuck's sake!

My dick jerked against the soft sheet. It clearly wasn't getting the message that it wasn't going to be seeing any action with the two beauties. *How can it, when your head is conjuring up image after image of what you'd like to do to the pair?*

I groaned and rolled over, throwing the pillow on the floor in frustration. I had a feeling it was going to be a long night. What kind of stupid idiot researches BDSM sites before going to bed? Yeah, that would be me. My lips clamped together as I tried to convince myself that it had all been for research purposes, that I'd simply been looking for ideas for the furniture for Richard's BDSM club. No, I hadn't spent hours thinking about things I could make to use on... *fucking hell.*

My dick twitched again and I gave up on ignoring it, throwing the covers off my naked body.

The darkness made it impossible to see, but I didn't need light when my dick was achingly hard and dripping over my stomach. Sweeping my fingers through the pre-cum, I used it to lube up my dick. My hand glided along the length of my dick, groaning at the slick feeling.

Air hissed out between my teeth as I scraped a fingernail over my wet slit, waves of pleasure spreading down into my balls. I undulated against the dampening sheet as I rubbed slick fingertips over the bulbous head. My dick throbbed, leaking in appreciation of my touch. I gathered more pre-cum, my dick pulsing in time to the beat of my heart as I stroked from base to tip, squeezing the head with each pass to release more liquid. My mind drifted to a pair of innocent violet eyes, a pair of eyes that would surely beg.

That air of innocence... was it real or fake?

I firmly shoved the unease accompanying the question aside as another crossed my mind. Would he be eager to be taught how to please a man?

Sweat gathered on my brow as my hand continued its slow strokes to thoughts of how I could teach Gwil to pleasure me, to suck my cock between those lush lips into, what I'd bet my last pound would be a heavenly mouth.

Would the other man be jealous or would he be eager to watch?

Sparks of liquid desire spread through my body, my balls tightening painfully with a sweet ache. Lowering my other hand, I cupped them, tugging on them to increase the pleasure. At the feel of my impending orgasm, I strained against the damp covers.

A noise had me jerking upright, my hand slipping from my cock despite its disapproval. My head tilted as I strained to hear past the whooshing sound in my ears.

What was that? The unfamiliar noise came again, my chest heaving. I shook my head, my eyes straining to see in the darkness. Had Sonny come back? Was he looking to take the remaining few things of value I had? Recalling the fact that the keys for the car were on the table downstairs, along with my wallet, I got up. Driven by the need to stop Sonny, I stalked naked towards the bedroom door. Taking a deep breath to try and clear my head, I silently opened the door.

Stepping quietly into the hallway, I froze at the sound of footsteps moving around downstairs.

How dare the fuckers break in and try and steal from me! Anger burned a hot path through me, leaving me shaking. My hands clenched into fists as I took to the stairs.

Whatever desire I'd previously felt was forgotten in my haste to stop whoever had dared to come into my premises. They were going to get more than they bargained for. Making no sound, I tiptoed down the stairs. At the bottom, I stopped, straining to hear exactly where they were in the building.

The whooshing in my ears made it difficult to hear, my lungs burning with the need to breathe deeply as I held my breath. I walked over to the open doorway of the shop illuminated by the street lights outside counting off the number of steps.

Air left my body so fast that my chest heaved, my eyes widening for a second before narrowing on the silver hair glinting in the light. There was the sound of a whimper,

Gwil appearing a second later. My heart pounded in a bid to escape my chest as questions clamoured in my brain.

Were these men trying to steal from me? Was that why they'd followed me? Were they after things they could pinch? I took in their scruffy appearances, my chest aching for a moment before I hardened my heart to the stupid thoughts I was having.

You are a foolish old man!

I marched into the room, the berating too similar to the one I'd given myself after Sonny had left. Fists balled, I fired an intimidating stare at both of them. "What do you think you're doing?" I growled with menace.

They swung around to face me and then froze. Blondie recovered first, his eyes growing to the size of dinner plates as his gaze lowered. His scrutiny felt like a caress as it travelled over my body.

Fuck, I'm still naked!

The thought was quickly followed by a wave of desire as Blondie eyed my dick with a hungry stare, licking his lips at the same time. My flagging arousal took notice pulsing with a renewed vigour.

The sound of an indrawn breath drew my gaze away from Blondie and over to the raven-haired beauty stood at his side. His face showed fear, yet there was a yearning in his violet eyes as well that left me fighting the urge to reassure him that everything was going to be alright.

Stop being such a fucking walkover. These men were going to rob you blind.

The fingernails of my clenched hands dug into the flesh of my palms, the bite of pain helping me to pull myself together. The longer they remained silent, the more the tension grew, along with my dick.

Gwil's hands fluttered at his sides but his gaze remained

on me. I eyed both men. How did I teach them a lesson they'd never forget?

You know what you want.

No! No.

The second 'no' ran through my head with less conviction, my cock hardening further and a drip of pre-cum showing these two men just how much I enjoyed them looking at me.

Sucking in a breath, I took a moment to collect my thoughts, attempting to reign in both my temper and my arousal. "Are either of you going to explain what the fuck you're doing in here before I call the police and have you arrested for breaking and entering?"

Blondie shuddered and one of my brows quirked. Was it the threat or my Dom voice that had made him quake like that? I wasn't convinced it was just the threat as my gaze swept down his body. The bulge in his jeans spoke volumes. I switched my attention to Gwil, who was facing a similar predicament.

The two warring sides of me hummed in agreement at the potential for what I could do.

You are not a monster! Let them go and leave it alone.

I shut out the voice of reason and took a step closer. The scent of my own arousal became more pungent in the warm room, my dick continuing to show how much the situation was affecting me.

Both men remained rooted to the spot, neither appearing to take a breath as I lifted my hands and cupped the back of their necks. The hair beneath my palms felt like spun silk, my fingers tightening. I inhaled, regretting it when I was met with an unwashed, stale scent. My nose wrinkled as I held the two men captive. "Are we going to keep up the silent treatment? Because I can assure you that

I have ways of making you talk to me. Now, are we going to do this the easy way, or the hard way? Which one of you is going to tell me why you've broken into my shop?"

As both men lowered their gazes and remained silent, my head filled with possibilities. Blondie chewed on his lower lip while Gwil's chin trembled. What was I going to do with them?

My dick stood proud, as if reaching out to the two men in offering. The head of it glistened, my slick pre-cum catching what little light filtered into the room. I watched Blondie carefully as he eyed me hungrily, his lower lip becoming swollen beneath the assault of his small, pearly-white teeth.

CHAPTER SIX

Gwil

The hairs on the back of my neck had alerted me to the man's presence. What I hadn't been prepared for when I'd whirled around was for everything else in the room to disappear at the sight of the gloriously naked body in front of me. My blood had pooled in my groin, bringing the arousal back to life that had started in the alleyway with Benidic.

Benidic was as silent as me as I struggled with my conflicting thoughts, the cock waving at me making it difficult to focus on what might happen next. My arse clenched, feeling empty. There was an ever-growing need in me that felt as if it was trying to claw its way out of my very being. Fear of the unknown clogged my throat, my hands fluttering at my sides with the need to touch.

You do not want to do that!

Oh, by the Elvedom, I do.

The man's threats did little to assuage the need. It was only when he stepped closer and took hold of my neck that panic kicked in. The long, lean fingers dug painfully into my flesh when neither of us answered his question. Yet, the touch of his hand felt oddly comforting, the same as Benidic's always had.

This man is not Benidic. How do you know he won't harm you?

With no answer coming to mind, I lowered my eyelashes and cast a quick look in Benidic's direction. Any hope of Benidic answering started to fade when he appeared spellbound by the man's slick cock protruding from his body.

"As neither of you seem to be willing to answer me, I think it's time to show you both that I'm not messing around here. I've been taken advantage of one too many times, but no more." The hard edge to his voice and darkening expression made my mouth go dry.

Before I could come up with a response, he'd already marched us out into the hallway and past several doors before leading us into a room which smelt of wood and leather. My eyes didn't have time to adjust to the complete darkness before he spoke.

"Blondie, flick the light on there, to your left."

Benidic whimpered and then light flooded the room.

Blondie?

The thought disappeared along with all the air in the room. Whatever oxygen had been in my lungs stayed right where it was, captured, just as my gaze was by the things in the room. Blinking slowly, I tried to focus, but then wished I hadn't. I'd seen some of the contraptions before, but only in one of the forbidden books that Benidic had got from an Elf he'd never named.

I hadn't forgotten the way in which he'd talked excitedly about what they could possibly be. I chanced another glance at him. The gleam of lust in his eyes made my own arousal pulse and push against the fabric of my trousers. Oh dear lord, what had we got ourselves into?

The tingling of my lips from the kiss with Benidic in the alleyway increased at the thought of doing more than kissing his lips. The lusty desire on Benidic's face seemed to be contagious, my body starting to crave things it never had before.

The want, no not want, the *need*, to do what was forbidden in Elvedom left me breathless. We'd never been naked in front of each other as it was prohibited until the mating ritual. It was something neither of us had been inclined to change when we were at home. Yet here... Yeah, that was a different matter altogether.

It was shocking to recall how I'd have let Benidic do whatever he wanted to me in that dark alleyway as long as he'd kept on touching me. I was convinced that Benidic felt the release of the sexual energy which had been bound at home too. The chains of our own realm were broken now that we were no longer there. Right now, what with the sensations awakening every part of my body, I was struggling to work out whether that was a good or a bad thing.

It's bad.

Is it really?

There was no time to gather my thoughts and figure it out though, as we were marched across the room. The hand holding my neck never eased its punishing grip, tears springing to my eyes in response to the obvious displeasure we'd given the man. Needing to appease him, I didn't resist, not even when my stomach dropped as we halted in front of a contraption with restraints.

Stormy eyes turned in my direction, the pressure against the back of my neck increasing. I sucked my lower lip between my teeth to keep from crying out. "I want you to sit on this bench and not move, understand?" The man's gaze moved to the leather padded seat that, at its base, held several pieces of metal chain.

The raspy demand held a hint of steel so I nodded, not wanting to increase his displeasure.

He pushed me onto the black, leather seat, but in retrospect I was grateful as I started to shake at his next words. "Now Blondie, let's get you out of these clothes and get you situated so you can see exactly what happens to naughty subs."

What was a naughty sub and what happened to them?

Don't ask.

Bands of tightness encircled my chest as I watched the man strip a silent Benidic. His head was lowered in a submissive pose I wasn't used to seeing and it played havoc with my pulse rate. His long hair was bound into a bun at the back of his head with a piece of leather. The man's nostrils flared and I was reminded that we hadn't washed in days.

When Benidic offered no protest, my concern lessened as his body was revealed to me for the very first time. Once he was naked, the man hummed low in the back of his throat as if he approved. Benidic's translucent skin gleamed under the bright light, his hairless body long, lean and fully aroused.

Would I look the same?

A shiver raced down my spine, Benidic's arousal holding my gaze while I strained to do as I'd been told and sit still. The picture both men made, standing naked and aroused in front of me stole my breath away.

The man kicked Benidic's clothes away before taking a step closer to him. "You like being bad, don't you?" he growled, his long fingers pinching Benidic's chin and lifting it.

The man's naked desire turned my insides to jelly and with it came a longing that he might look at me the same way.

"Yes," Benidic answered in a breathy whisper. His eyelashes dropped as if he was trying to shield his thoughts, but his body betrayed him as he trembled, his long, thin cock leaking and dripping onto the wooden floor. The scent of his arousal mixed with the musky aroma coming off the man.

There was no doubt about what Benidic wanted. I could feel it deep inside me and I swallowed a sigh of resignation. There was something dark inside the man, beyond just his dominance, a craving that matched Benidic's. I could see it now in the depths of his stormy eyes, a reveal as to who he truly was.

What was my place in this? Would I be forgotten, tossed aside when the man gave Benidic what he wanted?

The tightening in my stomach increased.

Please don't abandon me, I pleaded silently, the fear undermining any semblance of control I might have had.

CHAPTER SEVEN

Drake

At the show of submissiveness, I struggled to swallow past my dry throat. A throat that had become like the Nevada Desert the moment I'd exposed all that glowing, pale skin. A thread of disappointment wound through me at not being able to see what he'd look like with all that glorious, silky hair curtaining his body. My fingers tingled from the memory of its feel in my hands.

Would his skin feel the same? I eyed his beautiful body, my brows rising. Did he wax his entire body? There was no sign of hair other than on his head. The tingling in my fingers increased with the need to find out if his translucent skin was as soft and smooth as it appeared under the lights. My grip tightened on his chin, fighting the temptation to reach down and find out.

Was I really going to do this?

Was I really going to take advantage of these two men when they were evidently down on their luck?

The questions kept on coming, but the man standing in front of me almost seemed to challenge me to answer honestly.

Fuck it. Where had being a decent guy ever got me? I wanted this so fucking much. Fuck, I wanted it more than I wanted to take my next breath. Acknowledging the depth of need, I took a deep inhale to centre myself as I looked over at the man who sat watching us.

Huge violet eyes seemed to take hold of my battered heart and squeeze it gently in a protective hold. My heart stuttered at the feelings, my teeth grinding together. Was I being foolish to let my dick take charge here?

There was no easy answer, his eyes holding something akin to fear in their depths, but intuitively I understood that it wasn't about what was taking place, but more that he might be excluded from it. From my years of being a Dom and a Daddy I understood need, and this boy wanted what both Blondie and I could offer him: our undivided attention.

He might not know it yet but he had nothing to worry about. I craved the light and the dark in equal measures and he was as vital to me as the blood running through my veins.

Seconds ticked by and I understood that I'd been delaying the inevitable from the first moment I'd seen these men inside my shop. I looked at the pillory behind Blondie, taking a breath and then another. Releasing Blondie's chin, I guided him over to the handmade device that would hold him captive while I decided what his punishment should be.

The sound of his laboured breathing filled the silent room, but not once did he show reluctance. "Kneel on the pad and lean your chest against the metal frame." Only when he'd done as I asked, did I continue to explain what was about to happen.

"Put your face into the round hole." Taking the soft leather straps which hung from the handcrafted frame, I tethered his neck to the metal, gently tugging the few strands of hair that had escaped his bun and become trapped under the leather free. Once I was happy with the neck binding, I shifted back a little. "Put your arms behind your back."

This time there was a noticeable hesitation, his chest rising and falling in a fast staccato before he did as I'd asked. Only once he'd clasped his hands together did I select the leather straps I wanted to use. The collection of things I'd bought and made over the years was displayed on the back wall of the room. It was an alluring sight with whips, canes, floggers, masks, restraints and so much more sat on shelves or hanging from hooks. As my intrigue had increased, so had my collection of different instruments, all of which I loved to play with.

I stood and contemplated what I wanted, using the simple task to help centre me. A smile spread across my face as I reached for the two specially made pieces of dark-red leather imagining what they would look like against Blondie's milky skin. There were hooks on one end and on the other a belt fastening. When they were wound around the arms to hold them together the buckle restricted movement or prevented it completely depending on what the Dom's wishes were.

There was something about Blondie that made me want to push to see where his boundaries lay. He screamed novice, yet I wasn't totally convinced by that given the way he'd offered up his submission so easily. It spoke of a deeper understanding. Although, I wasn't sure if it was because he'd practiced it or if it was just instinctual. His movements were so fluid and his posture so perfect that it was a difficult call.

Going with my gut instinct, I decided to immobilise him

completely to see how he'd cope. I turned to face the men, both of them having remained where I'd put them. A warm satisfaction spread through me and I struggled not to show how much both men were pleasing me.

It's not about them pleasing you, remember. It's about finding out what they were doing in your shop.

My sigh was internal as I walked back over to Blondie and got my head back in the game. Once the hooks were slotted into the metal rings at the side of the neck brace, I made brief work of crisscrossing the leather around his arms until he had no movement in either of them. Then I buckled the ends together and tugged to check he couldn't move. A spark shot through my body as I touched his hands to check his circulation and I jerked back, my body humming at the strange sensation.

Struggling to regain the sense of calm from earlier, I forced myself to focus on the fact that I'd been right about the red leather complimenting his pale flesh. My gaze lingered for a moment until I felt able to move to shackle his ankles to the bench. I considered using a spreader bar, but discarded the thought as I spread his legs and discovered that they touched the edges of the padded stool he knelt on without the aid of a metal bar.

This time, there was no strange sensation from touching his skin and I released a quiet breath. My dick throbbed in approval at the sight of him fully tethered to the pillory as I stood. I circled him slowly, stopping in front of him. His thin cock stood proud and gleaming between the metal bars of the frame, his arousal showing no signs of flagging from what I'd done to him. My heart soared at my instincts being correct. The man was a true sub at heart.

That means nothing, you haven't started yet.

My inner voice had me questioning whether Blondie would be able to take everything I dished out, the Dom in me considering the need to give Blondie a safe word.

Did he deserve a safe word?

Every sub deserves that.

They broke into my home, into my place of business.

Reminding myself of that fact drowned out any thoughts of giving him a safe word. The men had tried to steal from me, so didn't they deserve everything they got?

My hands shook as I got close enough to Blondie to feel his hot breath on the tip of my dick. His eyes were hooded as his dick jerked.

"You want to suck my cock, Blondie? You want to taste me on your pretty lips? Do you want me to make you choke on my dick while I force it down your throat?" I rasped, struggling to get the words out past the dryness in my throat. There was a low whimper from Blondie and I glanced over at Gwil, but his gaze was fixed on Blondie.

"Come here, Gwil." The eagerness with which he moved off the bench was distracting. But then warm, wet lips touched the tip of my cock. I exhaled in a rush, bracing my knees to stop them from shaking as I turned my attention back to Blondie. He'd pushed himself forward, enough to be able to manoeuvre his face between the metal ring, his body straining. The leather binding had tightened around his neck, his pale skin flushing a deep red. He seemed unaware that he was cutting off his own air supply as his lips moved eagerly over the tip of my cock.

My jaw clenched at the effort it took to pull far enough away that he couldn't reach me. My chest heaved as I eyed Blondie, who showed no remorse for what he'd just done. "You are the sub here. I'm your master. Did I say you could touch me?" I ground out, struggling with a confusing mixture of emotions which ran amok inside me. The Dom wanted to show him who was in charge, yet the need to take care of him battled with the desire to make him pay. It was a total mindfuck.

Get a fucking grip.

CHAPTER EIGHT

Benidic

Oh to the heavens!

I blamed my lightheadedness on the lack of air in my lungs. It could be the only explanation for the hare-brained idea of moving my head forward in order to taste the cock that had been tempting me.

When the man in front of me had hummed in pleasure from my touch, my soul had sung with a joy it had never known before. Even using magic had never given me the sense of completeness which had swept over me from being tied to this contraption. Waves of dizziness continued to sweep through me. Although with my head and body in conflict at what was happening, I wasn't sure if it was from fear or excitement.

From the moment we'd used magic to open the locks and entered the back of the shop, I'd known that my instincts had been correct. There was something we could do to help this man. Although, I wasn't convinced it was what we were currently doing. But the minute I'd seen him naked and aroused, there'd been no magic in the universe which would have stopped me from seeing the emotions in the depths of his stormy eyes as he'd watched Gwil and me.

Had I lost my mind? Had being on Earth taken away all my common sense?

Tell him no. Do it now before this goes any further.

It's already gone too far, for heaven's sake.

I shut my eyes, trying to block out the sight in front of me. That was nigh on impossible though, given the lingering taste of pre-cum on my lips. Dear Elvedom, why did you make us wait so long to experience this?

They don't do depravity, remember?

I shuddered, recalling the secret meeting with the Elf who'd given me a book on bondage and sadism. When I'd heard that he had access to one. It was strictly forbidden for Elves to visit the human realm. Yet, when I'd questioned him I'd got the distinct impression that he was a frequent visitor.

The Elf in question was of age and bonded to another, but he'd kept his mate out of sight on the two occasions I'd visited. The first time I'd gone to discuss what I'd heard, and the second to deliver the bribe he'd required for my silence. I'd never told Gwil how I'd obtained the book. He'd been scared enough by its contents. The book had only made me more unsettled and sensing that there was something vital to my being missing. For days afterwards, I'd had to block out the concern in Gwil's eyes as he pondered what the future might hold for us.

It seemed he should have worried less about that and more about keeping out of trouble.

But you wouldn't be here now, experiencing this, if he had.

At a tug on the strap around my neck, I opened my eyes, blinking twice. I must have zoned out longer than I'd thought because Gwil was... *naked*. He was naked! Holy Elvedom! How had I missed that? His beautiful, willowy body was mere inches from my face.

When it hit me that I could do nothing to protect him, I started to struggle in the restraints, the urge to defend him too persistent to ignore. The man laughed as I was left gasping for breath, my whole body shaking with the effort. But all I achieved was raw skin, burned by the metal and leather bindings.

A hollowness I'd never experienced before filled my chest and I cursed myself seven ways to hell and back. I was so lost in my misery that it took a while to register the state of Gwil's body. I stilled, the other man completely forgotten, my gaze fixed on Gwil's groin.

Did he want this too?

His dick, which was in much the same state as mine, said yes, but he appeared conflicted too, his normally smooth brow holding deep furrows. I locked my gaze on his, begging him with damp eyes to forgive me. The sorrow in his eyes stole my breath away, but there was also acceptance for whatever was about to happen.

Why did you think it was okay to touch the man's cock?

Was he going to make Gwil pay for my actions?

I swallowed a groan, trying to keep the images of that same cock out of my head. I couldn't see the man in question, but I could still smell his musky, masculine aroma, my heart rate accelerating.

A few seconds later, I registered the weight of his gaze on my flesh, almost like an invisible pressure. Under the weight of it, I sagged against the metal. A rough palm stroked down my flank before holding my hip in a bruising grip. I froze, barely able to take a breath, sparks of desire flooding through me. I kept my eyes locked on Gwil in the desperate hope that it might stop me from exploding into a million pieces at the touch.

"Oh Gods," I cried out as the other hand came down heavily against my arse delivering a stinging blow which blurred my vision. My body tried to arch, tried to move, but it was to no avail, a mewl passing my dry lips as my limbs strained in an attempt to break free of the restraints.

The next slap rang out loudly, the sound adding to my cock's torment. Delicious licks of desire spread to my channel, the next blow feeling almost like he'd touched my cock directly.

Tears slid down my cheeks, blinding me. Immense heat spread through my body as nerve endings fired to life as I rejoiced at the new feelings flooding through me. Pain melded into something more life affirming, my mind commanding my body to stop fighting and focus solely on the blows raining down on my arse.

Then, it was as if someone had turned on a light inside me and all I was left with was soaring pleasure. It filled the whole of my body, blocking out everything else. "Ohhhhh Elvedommmmm," I cried mindlessly, my cock aching. Then the ache turned into an intense burning which blew my brain to smithereens. The need for something, anything to touch my dick rocketed through me and became all I could focus on.

"Gwil, touch me," I howled in distress, my hands clenching and unclenching uselessly.

"Don't you dare," came a growled response that made me cry out.

"Oh please, please, anything, please... master," I begged, not caring if I sounded like a rambling idiot. The blows continued and I hung suspended in an erotic hell, my body straining to reach an unseen pinnacle with no sense of how to get there. It was right there though. I could feel it just within my grasp.

I blinked furiously, trying to see through blurry eyes, needing Gwil to do as I'd asked. He was stood so temptingly close, his hands fluttering at his sides and his face conflicted as he moved his gaze back and forth between me and the man, who was continuing to spank my painfully tender backside.

I strained against nothing, air teasing the damp tip of my cock. The goddamn thing bucked and jerked with each slap, but it still wasn't enough.

The spanking stopped as quickly as it had started, my chest heaving as I slumped against the frame holding me captive. I undulated, rocking back and forth as much as the bindings would allow, seeking anything which would ease the pleasure as the heat from my arse spread down my channel, into my sac and up to the tip of my dick. Even without the painful stimulus, my dick continued to thrum and pulse to the beat of my heart.

"I get to decide when you come. You've done nothing to deserve that, have you, sub?" The man moved into my line of sight as he spoke. His voice was like silk, sliding erotically over my flesh which only added to my torment.

I licked my dry lips as he moved over to Gwil, taking hold of his arm to guide him to the bench a couple of feet away. When he sat and pulled Gwil between his large, hairy thighs, a spurt of jealousy took my breath away. It only increased as he nudged Gwil's legs apart before pulling him down onto his lap.

I gulped at the sight of the large purple head of his cock protruding from underneath Gwil's balls. In contrast with Gwil's milky skin, it looked obscene. My arse clenched at the thought of what it might feel like to feel that flesh rub against my skin in the same way.

Gwil's eyes hooded as a large, tanned hand wrapped firmly around his dick, a dark flush of colour flooding his cheeks. His long, raven hair hung loosely over his shoulders and an almost dreamy expression appeared on his face taking my breath away.

Gwil's hips moved and his splayed thighs shook.

Was he rubbing himself against the man's cock?

My body reacted instantly to the idea, the spurt of jealousy disappearing beneath a need to see what the man would do to Gwil while I watched. Stormy eyes met mine over the top of Gwil's head as if he could read my thoughts.

"Now, which one of you wants to tell me what you're doing in my home?" he rasped. His hand stroked gently up Gwil's dick. When he'd reached the top, he gave it a squeeze, a bead of pre-cum pearling on the tip, my tongue coming out instinctively, wanting to taste.

"Ohhhh," Gwil groaned. His eyelids fluttered closed and his mouth hung open, a look of ecstasy on his face.

The groan turned to a moan of distress as the man let go of his dick. He placed the tip of his finger with the pre-cum on it next to Gwil's lips, his gaze still on me.

"Suck it clean for, Daddy," he encouraged in a soft voice.

Daddy?

My heart fluttered in my chest. Was this what the book had meant by Daddy kink?

I stopped thinking about it at the sight of Gwil's heavy-lidded desirous gaze as his eyes opened and, without any hesitation, he leant forward and did as he was told. He whimpered as he sucked the thick digit between his lips, his cheeks hollowing to show how much he was enjoying the taste.

Was this what he needed... a Daddy?

Warmth spread through me. I'd always known Gwil wanted to be nurtured so in a way I recognised what it was the man was giving him.

I panted, my hips moving restlessly, an ache throbbing through my entire body in response to the erotic display,

"Let go, Gwil. Let Daddy give you more."

Gwil immediately did as he was told and I watched in fascination as his body relaxed back, his dark head resting on the man's large shoulder. The man had gone back to stroking him from base to tip. Several more beads of pre-cum appeared as he slicked up his finger before moving it back to Gwil's willing mouth.

A sheen of sweat covered Gwil's face, his entire body writhing against the man behind him. Slurping sounds filled the room as he sucked enthusiastically on the finger in his mouth. It was the large, angry-looking cock which strained beneath Gwil's moving body that captured my attention though.

"Please, please let me taste... Master," I begged unashamedly, recalling that was how he'd referred to himself.

CHAPTER NINE

Drake

The sexual energy in the room buzzed against my skin in ways it never had before. I'd played with others too many times to count, but not once had I felt an electrical charge like this. What was different about these two?

It's because these men are yours. The voice whispered in my mind and I swallowed the ball of panic that arose as I realised it wasn't my own. It took all of my willpower not to throw the writhing man off my lap as I glanced quickly around the room. It looked the same as it always did. Yet, I sensed there was... there was what?

What the fuck was going on? Were these two fucking with me somehow? Playing some sort of mind game?

Give over, how can they project a voice in your head? You're losing your mind.

The hungry mouth sucking on my finger and the wanton silver eyes watching us reminded me what I was meant to be doing: getting answers and then kicking them out. My gut clenched though at the thought of making either man leave. *Ever!*

There was no chance to think about what I should do, not with Blondie begging, "Please, please let me taste... Master."

The way Master tripped off his tongue felt as if he was sat between my thighs licking my cock. It bucked, Gwil's thighs instinctively closing around me, his hips rocking faster as his own juices slid between us and acted like lube.

My groan of pleasure echoed around the room as Gwil continued to squeeze my hard length through the channel created by his thighs. He released my saliva-slicked finger, his hands lifting as he twisted around so that I could see his face. Soft fingers touched my cheeks, my whole body tensing at the intense feelings that accompanied the gentle touch. It was the same sensation I'd felt earlier when I'd touched Blondie's hands, only this time it made my entire body tremble.

If I'd had any thoughts of stopping him from touching me, I was powerless to do so when he turned his violet eyes on me. The sheer want in them was a punch to the gut and I struggled to breathe.

"D-Daddy, let Benidic taste you. Don't let him suffer. I'll tell you anything you want to know. I swear I will." His chin wobbled, his eyes sheening with tears. I could see honesty in the depths of his gaze so I was powerless to resist his request.

Be honest, you want Blondie's mouth on you.

I was too long in the tooth to ignore the truth so I carefully lowered Gwil to the floor. The sense of loss as his hands dropped from my face was instantaneous and I had to swallow a demand for him to touch me again.

What the fuck is wrong with me?

This pair had fucking stolen my sanity, that's what was wrong with me.

I shook off the feeling that I might be losing my mind as I stood next to Gwil. Reluctant to touch his hands again, I steered him over to Blondie by the elbow. Not Blondie… Benidic.

Only once Gwil was stood to the side of Benidic, did I move to the other side of the pillory. Gwil's brows rose and he chewed his lower lip between his teeth. His gaze lowered to Benidic's sweaty face before moving back to me.

"He wanted to taste us both. That's right, isn't it, Benidic?" I stroked a hand over his head, the silky feel of his hair making my fingers tingle.

"Yes, yes please."

He whimpered as my fingers dug into his scalp. "Yes please…?"

"Yes please, Master," he corrected, sounding breathless.

Gwil's cock bucked, his lust-laden gaze locked on mine. "Step closer and place your cock next to Benidic's mouth, but don't touch him," I growled, doing the same.

The tip of my slick dick brushed sensually against Gwil's. He trembled, his mouth hanging open and whimpers falling from his lips that did crazy things to my heart. Tiny licks of pleasure skittered along the length of my arousal stoking the fire higher as Benidic's warm breath touched my flesh.

The warm, wet caresses from touching Gwil's leaking shaft hardened my already stiff length. It swelled and throbbed in time to my heartbeat as I took hold of the base and increased the slow rolling motion of my hips.

Sounds of heavy breathing, mixed with moans and whimpers, filled the room. The prolonged arousal caused my sac to tighten, alerting me to the fact that I wouldn't last much longer as the tingling at the base of my spine increased. Playtime was over.

"Poke out your tongue, Benidic," I ground out through clenched teeth. At the sight of his pale pink tongue lapping at both of our dicks, my eyes hooded. Colour flooded his face as he strained to get closer, to touch more.

Taking pity on him, I encouraged Gwil to come closer and to twist his body around so that Benidic could reach his cock and suck it into his mouth. The moment those lush lips enclosed Gwil, he cried out, his whole body shaking. He closed his eyes and swayed, his arms moving restlessly at his sides. His face was a mask of rapture, giving him a blissed-out expression.

Fuck, he was stunning! My hand wrapped around the base of my dick and moved roughly along my length in time to each suck given to the head of Gwil's dick by Benidic.

Benidic's hips jerked in an uncoordinated rhythm as if he had no idea what to do with his body. Before I knew it though, my own orgasm was starting to trickle up from my balls to my cock.

Benidic's hungry gaze met mine and it was game over. I stepped closer, thrusting my cock through his clenched fingers. His eyes pleaded and I stroked faster, my chest straining as I lost the ability to take a breath, my dick throbbing painfully. My body spasmed, hot cum spurting out and hitting Gwil's cock and Benidic's face. Both men mewled in unison as my dick continued to pump hot spurts of cum over them, claiming them as mine. The pearly liquid dripped off Benidic's face and landed on Gwil's dick. There was no time for it to slide off though as Benidic's greedy tongue lapped it up.

Fucking hell!

"You're mine now," I roared, throwing my head back as the orgasm refused to release me from its grip.

Sweat poured off me as my aching balls released. Once

my brain was back online, I held on to the pillory, staring at the two men.

Gwil's whole body was trembling, his cock flaccid. Benidic looked replete, even though his face was a sticky mess. When my gaze dropped, I found out why, a chuckle escaping before I could stop it as I took in the mess on the floor and over Gwil's legs.

Well, that wouldn't do. I turned my attention back to Benidic, bending down so that we were eye to eye. "Did you come without permission, sub?"

His nostrils flared but he lowered his gaze. "Yes... Master. But... it's not my fault. I couldn't help it," he rushed to say, his face losing its happy glow of moments ago.

I pinched his chin. "Look at me," I commanded. Once his eyes were on me, I continued. "A trained sub knows better. How is it not your fault?" I frowned as the colour drained from his face.

"I... I... we... I," tears leaked from his eyes as they implored me, but to do what I had no idea.

"We've never known pleasure like this," Gwil whispered.

I stared at him. "What do you mean? You've never done a BDSM scene before? Or do you mean something else?" The scepticism was clear in my voice.

"We've never done anything before... ever... none of it." His gaze swept the room, his hands moving restlessly at his sides.

I wanted to accuse him of lying, but there was a ring of truth in there that I couldn't ignore. I stood and stepped back, the jackhammer that had replaced my heart making it nigh on impossible to breathe. My heart beat up into my throat, my eyes widening on both men. Benidic closed his eyes, but not before I saw what looked like shame in their depths.

Were these two men... virgins?

How was that possible in this day and age?

It can't be.

I got a sinking feeling in the pit of my stomach as I stared at both men.

What the fuck have I just done?

CHAPTER TEN

Gwil

Inhaling the scent of the body wash, I slicked my hands with it before cleaning my chest. The glorious hot water beating down on my body was heaven. Days of washing only the bits that mattered with icy cold water in a tiny sink had not been fun. So I wallowed in this new luxury that I'd taken for granted at home.

Feeling the weight of the gaze from the man who stood outside the shower, I sped up. After my confession, I thought I'd messed up for sure, the disbelief from the man replaced with a look of suspicion as he'd silently untied Benidic.

The gentle way he'd freed him had been at odds with the gruff tone he'd used when he'd insisted that we go and wash before... *before what?* Before he called the police? Before he kicked us back out onto the streets?

He'd said nothing more to either of us as he'd escorted us into a huge bathroom. I kept my eyelashes lowered, flicking a quick glance every now and again at the still naked man as he leaned against the marble counter that housed two sinks. The mirror behind him showed a reflection of my body. I exhaled shakily at what I looked like stood next to Benidic.

Our stature was similar, but his muscles were more defined from years of fighting. His long hair looked darker now that it was wet and clinging to his soapy body. His limp cock lay nestled between his legs as he stood facing the man. It was almost as if he was trying to entice him to do more than just stare at us.

Did I want more?

My cock twitched at the memory of his firm hand stroking me, of the taste of my cum on his finger. The rough texture of his skin had rasped against my tongue and had been far more arousing than I would have expected. Not that sex had been something I'd given much thought to, not until we'd arrived in the human world. Now it seemed to be all I could think about.

What about when he called himself Daddy? You can't stop thinking about that too.

Some of the content in the book Benidic had commandeered in Elvedom had started to make sense. Any suspicion that I might have been interested in the same things as Benidic had been proven wrong in the room downstairs. The sight of Benidic tied up, watching the man touch me as I'd called him Daddy was something I'd never forget. I'd never thought of myself as a sexual being before, but in that room I'd craved things I wasn't sure I'd be able to lock away again once we returned home.

The twitching in my cock became more evident as it started to plump, my fingernails digging into my palms in order to resist the urge to stroke myself, to feel the shocking, mind-bending pleasure I'd got from both of these men again. I wanted to feel Benidic's lips and his tongue as he sucked whatever brains I had left right out of my cock.

Fuck. The beating of my heart made my ears buzz, a wave of dizziness rendering me breathless.

I loved Benidic with all my soul. Yet when this man touched me, it felt like a missing piece had returned, one I wasn't even aware had been taken. How could that be? How was it possible to feel something like that for a stranger?

"Whatever are you thinking about, Gwil?"

I was pulled from my thoughts, realising that I'd been openly staring at the man in question. The way he spoke demanded that I answer honestly, but how was I supposed to explain without giving too much away? I sighed in frustration.

"Answer Daddy, unless you want to find your bottom as red as Benidic's." His dark brows rose as he took the three steps needed to bring him closer to the glass shower door that separated us.

I glanced over at Benidic as he gave a low moan. He'd turned side-on, and I could see the effect the conversation was having on him as he touched his still blood-red arse cheeks. His fingers moved tentatively over the flesh, the skin on my own arse warming at the sight. Oh dear lord! What was wrong with me? I stepped back in a panic, stopping as I pressed up against the cool, wet tiles.

I shook my head as the door of the shower opened, a waft of cold air filling the large cubicle. "Oh noooooo!" I held my hands up as he stepped inside and shut the door. His appealing expression did little to help my cock.

"Are you going to answer, Daddy?" he growled. The devilish glint in his eyes increased as he took hold of my outstretched hands, keeping them captive in his.

His eyes widened as he stared down at our joined hands as if he was seeing them for the very first time. Magic, that had been absent until the man had touched me downstairs, hummed to life again. I focused on it and a spark of light flared between us. Benidic exhaled noisily, his body pressing against my side as I didn't dare look away.

Colours I associated with my magic haloed the man in front of me, bathing him in a purple, lilac and violet hue. His eyes hooded as his dark lashes fluttered. Desire pulsed between the three of us, Benidic's magic—an array of reds, melding with mine. The moment felt endless, my chest filling with the familiar feel of my magic. I breathed easy for the first time in days.

It was only the sensation of Benidic's cock moving restlessly against my hip that forced me to break the connection. The scent of arousal coming off both men in waves was too strong to ignore. With the spell broken, the man shook his head, his eyes narrowing on both of us.

"What... the... ever-loving... fuck... was... that?"

Benidic didn't seem to hear the threat in the man's voice as he rubbed harder and faster against my slicked-up skin. He appeared completely unaware of the trouble brewing in the stormy eyes which glared at us both.

"Benidic, what did I say downstairs?" the man ground out, sounding furious as he let go of my hands in order to pull Benidic off me. "The pair of you, out of the shower *now*. The two of you should come with a fucking warning label."

The last part was said with so much anger that I sagged under the weight of it knowing that I'd caused it. "I'm sorry... Daddy," I mumbled through my tears, watching him stiffen as he switched off the shower and pushed Benidic through the cubicle door he'd just opened.

With a heavy heart, I stepped out behind them, waiting to see if he'd do as he'd promised and punish me. Towels were tossed at both Benidic and myself. The man took another to swipe at his body. The need to try and appease him driving sane thoughts from my head, I hesitantly walked over to him.

For the love of Elvedom what are you doing?

I clutched the towel as I took a deep breath before lifting it and gently moving it over his damp skin.

His hands dropped to his sides, the mask slipping into place on his face making it impossible for me to read him. Taking his silence and the fact he hadn't pushed me away as permission, I carried on. The only sound in the room was heavy breathing as I knelt to dry his thick, hairy legs. My gaze was drawn to his groin as I lifted my head. Although his cock wasn't hard, it was plumper than it had been when I'd started. Had I done that?

I tilted my head back and continued to eye his cock. Dark hair encircled its base and covered his sac. Elf bodies were hairless, or so I'd always been told. Up until today, the only one I'd seen before was my own, so it was good to know that Benidic was the same. It seemed this was not the case when it came to human men. His cock thickened and lengthened further under my continued perusal.

"Jesus, what is it with you two? You're acting like you've never seen a naked body before," he growled out.

Heat spread up my neck, making it impossible to hide my discomfort at how close he was to the truth. But before I could respond, his hand lowered to grasp his cock. He gave it a lazy stroke before holding it in the direction of my mouth.

Oh my!

"Can I taste it... Daddy?" I begged, unable to stop the words from pouring out of my mouth. The slit of his dick gleamed beneath the lights and I swallowed hard in anticipation.

"Fuck, yes!"

If I'd had time I might have sagged in relief, but my brain was way ahead of me needing no further prompting. I opened my lips, inhaling his scent as my mouth slid down his length. It felt like silk-encased steel as it rubbed against my tongue stretching my mouth to full capacity. Unprepared for the touch at the back of my throat, I coughed and gagged. But as I went to pull back a hand locked into place at the back of my head and held me in place.

My eyes streamed and saliva dripped out of my mouth as I found it impossible to swallow.

"You asked Daddy to taste, now take it like a good boy. Relax your throat." The softness in his voice was in complete contrast to the dark, feral look on his face as he stared down at me. Needing to please him, I tried to relax my throat.

I coughed and choked, more saliva sliding off my chin to hit my chest. My hands scrabbled on his thighs, my chest heaving, a wave of panic taking hold at the thought of not being able to catch my breath.

"Breathe through your nose. Listen to Daddy. That's it, breathe through your nose." His cock swelled further in my mouth as I obeyed, pleasure racing through me at the knowledge that by doing as he'd asked I'd given him pleasure. Using the knowledge to keep me from panicking again, I grasped his thighs, shifting up to try and figure out a better angle. It worked, the cock no longer feeling like it was going to choke me, my other senses starting to take notice.

As If I'd silently called to Benidic, his warm, clean-scented body pressed to my back, his arms wrapping around me. His soft hands massaged my chest as if he was encouraging air into my body. The calm I always got from his touch settled over me. Although this time there was something else mixed with it, a sexual tension that hummed through me. My whole body thrummed with light and energy as I was surrounded by these two men, by the scent of their aroused bodies. It was intoxicating, maddening and life affirming like nothing ever had been before. Magic flowed through me and my hands warmed. I stroked the solid thighs I had hold of, needing to share the gift.

Was this what it was like to bond with a mate?

The thought disappeared beneath the effect of the pulsing magic, emotions increasing as they took charge.

CHAPTER ELEVEN

Drake

Standing at the end of my bed, I stared at the two sleeping men cuddled together in the middle of the mattress with their bare chests on display. Their faces looked so pure, so innocent in the early morning light coming through the crack in the curtains.

I scratched at my bristly jaw, the noise breaking the silence. Gwil shifted, the hand on Benidic's chest clenching before he settled again. My gaze was drawn to his swollen lips, my dick twitching at the memory of how they'd got that way. These two men were... were what? Unusual? Odd? Otherworldly?

The last thought caused my gut to clench. I swung around and left the room, leaving the door open so I would hear them if they tried to do a runner. I'd still not got any answers to my questions other than knowing their names.

Whose fault is that? Yours. That's who! If you'd stopped shoving your cock into that heavenly, inexperienced mouth for one minute, then you might have got answers!

Sighing, I went downstairs. I avoided looking through the open doorway of my playroom as I passed. I didn't need any more reminders right then. Considering my lack of sleep, all my tired brain wanted was some caffeine.

If I was going to find answers to what this pair's game was, I needed to screw my head back on. In all the previous times I'd played with men, I'd never once taken away their control, not without the use of contracts, safe words and an explicit understanding about the expectations of all involved. So what had happened last night?

It had been a clusterfuck of epic proportions where I'd broken every rule in the book. My gut twisted into ugly knots at the realisation that I wasn't sorry. In the harsh light of day, I couldn't hide from what I'd done.

Why hadn't I just rung the cops and had their arses taken to jail? *Because that was the last thing you wanted, admit it.*

"Who the fuck wouldn't want those two?" I muttered under my breath, stomping around the kitchen and building up a head of steam that I had no outlet for.

"You do have an outlet," whispered a voice that sounded much the same as the one I'd heard in my head the previous night. I swung around with my fists raised, ready to do battle with an unnamed foe.

"Show yourself," I growled at the empty room, not caring how ridiculous I might appear. My ears buzzed as if I'd been sat in the park next to a beehive too long.

I lowered my shaky arms. I'd clearly lived in London too fucking long and inhaled too much exhaust fumes from the streets. It had to be that, right? Weren't there studies that said it caused long term health problems?

You're just sleep deprived, that's all.

I latched on to the thought and refused to let it go, even when another part of me said differently. I'd gone more than two days without sleep before and never heard voices that weren't mine in my head. Maybe it was an age thing?

I groaned and rubbed my face.

Have you finished having a meltdown?

Swallowing a sigh, I walked over to the kitchen counter on unsteady legs, distracting my runaway brain with the simple task of making a pot of coffee. Cup in hand, I walked over to the large kitchen table to sit down. I stared at the black liquid in the cup but all I could see was Gwil's silky raven hair spread across my pillow.

Once he'd finished blowing my mind with what had to be one of the most inexperienced blow jobs I'd ever had, I'd been left with a pit of unease where my stomach used to be, reminding me of Gwil's confession in the playroom. Were they really that inexperienced?

The blow job had been sloppy and Gwil had used far more teeth than I was used to. He'd been uncoordinated, the same way he had when Benidic had pleasured him. It was as if he had no understanding of what to do with himself. Benidic wasn't much better when it came to BDSM etiquette. I found myself questioning again whether the way he behaved was more instinctual than experienced. He'd shown that when he'd rubbed himself against Gwil in an attempt to come. Much to his distress, I'd stopped him though.

Gwil hadn't been much better, what with his needy expression. Although he'd appeared to have more control over himself, managing to remain silent as I'd guided them both into my bedroom. Whereas Benidic had continued to whine until I'd retrieved a metal cock cage. His confused expression had again demonstrated a lack of understanding, bringing home to me the truth of what Gwil had spoken of.

A smile twitched on my lips at the memory of Benidic's

arousal having fled by the time I'd caged his dick, his expression showing only bewilderment. Then they'd both meekly got into my bed. As I had no other in the house, I'd been left with no other option but to give them mine. That was my excuse and I was sticking to it. It had nothing to do with my desire to have seen them there even before they'd broken into my shop.

That had been an hour ago. They'd fallen asleep almost immediately and it was only then that I'd taken the time to look at them without lust or anger. The dark circles under their eyes reminded me of how their clothes had smelt and my assumption of them being down on their luck. Were they homeless? Their clothes weren't cheap and nasty though. Yes, they smelt and they had some stains on them, but they were in far too good a condition to have been on the streets for a long time. Had they had problems with their family and been kicked out?

Maybe they'd shown off their freaky light show?

What was it with those bloody magic hands? How had they learnt to create electric sparks? My heart beat faster recalling how Gwil had rubbed my thighs while Benidic was plastered to Gwil's back watching him hungrily suck me dry. The light had been there then, I was sure of it. The only problem was, with Benidic all over Gwil, I'd had other things on my mind that had stopped me from questioning the light sparking from Gwil when he'd touched me. The sparks had set my blood on fire burning through me so fast that I was powerless against their onslaught and I'd come faster than a teenager.

And what about the rainbow show in the shower? I was sure I'd seen fucking colours floating around me. It was as if someone had created the Northern Lights in my bathroom.

How was that even possible? A spray of water reflecting the light, maybe?

Yeah, it really looked like that—not!

I'd never been closed to the possibility of such things, but that? Fuck! It wasn't so much the colour show, it was the way it had made me feel bloody invincible, like nothing could touch me.

My teeth raked over my lower lip as I continued to stare into the cup like it held the answers. I sat there until the cup was cold, not having taken even one sip while I tried to figure out what the hell was going on and what I should do next.

In the process of getting up to get a fresh cup of coffee, I paused, tilting my head to one side. Was that voices that I could hear?

I placed my cup down, walking barefoot down the hall and stopping at the bottom of the stairs.

"What are we going to do?" Gwil asked.

"Don't ask me, Gwil. You're not the one wearing this... contraption," Benidic whined.

"What you should do is get your backsides down these stairs, quick-smart," I bellowed, my lips twitching as two squeals followed my words. "Move it. The pair of you."

I remained at the bottom of the stairs, not disappointed when both men hurried to the top of the stairs naked. Benidic kept glancing down at his groin, his face conveying too many emotions for me to be able to catch them all.

They both stopped when they saw me standing at the bottom of the stairs. Gwil took hold of Benidic's hand and for a second, I thought I caught sight of a light glowing between their joined, hands but, in the blink of an eye, it had disappeared. Shaking off my unease, I pointed at them first and then down at the floor where I was standing.

Both men moved gracefully and completely in sync as they came down the stairs. My breath caught in my lungs at the beautiful picture they made. The hair curtaining their willowy frames only added to the allure, my mouth drying up.

The metal cage nestled between Benidic's thighs drew my gaze as it gleamed. The silver was almost the exact same colour as his eyes, and once again I was reminded of how I'd thought they looked *otherworldly*.

In the few seconds it took for them to reach me, my body had already become fully aroused, my dick tenting the joggers I'd thrown on earlier. Two pairs of hungry eyes dropped down, identical expressions revealing their excitement at my body's reaction to their nakedness.

This wouldn't do! Who the fuck was in control here?

Not you, evidently, came a snippy voice which thankfully sounded more like me than the other voice had.

Hopes of burying my cock inside either man was ignored as I turned around before glancing back at the men. "Stop looking at me like that. It's time you spilled your guts. Now follow me," I ground out through a jaw so clenched that it throbbed, determined that I wouldn't change my mind.

Needing a minute to calm the fuck down and control my unruly dick, I didn't wait to see if they'd followed. I palmed my cock and pushed it down, cursing under my breath as the unrepentant fucker bucked hard against my hand. Once we were in the kitchen, I glanced down at my groin. "Not happening, so quit bugging me."

At the sound of a cough behind me, I closed my eyes. Would I ever get a break?

CHAPTER TWELVE

Benidic

At Gwil's forced cough, I glanced from the man's broad back to him, my brow rising. Why was he coughing? Had he wanted to alert the man that we were right behind him when he'd been talking to... well, I wasn't at all sure who he'd been talking to. Himself, maybe? I did that myself from time to time when I wanted to figure stuff out and Gwil wasn't around.

I became distracted by the heavenly scent of coffee coming from somewhere in the room. My stomach growled as I glanced over to the counter. The man had turned by now and was eyeing us with suspicion in his stormy eyes.

His dark brows met in the middle of his forehead as he pointed to the table. "Take a seat on the far side. Do you want a drink? Something to eat?" he asked somewhat begrudgingly if his tone was anything to go by.

I nodded eagerly meeting his gaze. But as a dark brow lifted up questioningly heat flared in my cheeks and I lowered my gaze. "Yes Master," I answered carefully, trying not to peek from under my eyelashes to see if I'd read him right.

Gwil was rooted to the spot next to me uncertainty rolling off him in waves.

There was the sound of tutting followed by mumbled curses. "Sit, the pair of you. I'll make you some breakfast and then you can explain yourselves." His dominant stance and tone said it was pointless arguing.

Doing as he'd said, I tugged Gwil over to the table. Seeing the hard, wooden stools, I hesitated. I didn't want to put the dirty clothes we'd been wearing back on, but the thought of sitting naked while eating just seemed wrong.

Gwil appeared to be having the same thought. I squeezed his fingers reassuringly, not sure whether the intention was to give him a boost, or myself.

"Could we get dressed, please... Master?" If using the term Master gave him the same warm feeling as it gave me, then I hoped it would be enough to keep me in his good graces.

So far, I felt like I'd failed at every attempt at being what he wanted. The book hadn't included a whole heap of information about how to act with a Dominant. It had been more about the different types of kink in the human world, along with pictures of some of the equipment that could be used on a submissive.

"Ouccchhhh!" I cried out as my hair was grasped in a punishing grip. My dick bucked in its metal confines and it suddenly dawned on me what the thing was for. He didn't want me to get hard. Tears leaked out of my eyes without permission. Why didn't he want me to be aroused? My breath caught as all answers pointed towards him not being interested in me.

"I think you're trying to play games with me, little boy. But I'm wise to you. Do you think I didn't notice your hesitation when you called me Master?" His eyes pinned me in place, the storm brewing in their depths making my whole body thrum with excitement.

"I'm not, I swear, Master," I cried out.

"Then explain to me what a Master is?" The veiled threat was clear as he dared me to lie.

"He doesn't know. We don't know. You used that word and... and it somehow matches what Benidic has been searching for," Gwil whispered in a frightened voice.

I sagged, the grip on my hair tightening as the man switched his attention to Gwil.

"Explain yourself," he rasped.

I sensed Gwil even before I felt the heat of his body as he moved closer to me. "Benidic and I have been friends since birth. Sometimes I know him better than I know myself. He craves... what happened in that room last night. He needs something I can't give him... someone who'll let him embrace his darker side..." He trailed off, sounding tearful and utterly devastated by his own failings.

I wrenched my head back from the man's grip hard enough to see stars, but it gave me the few inches I needed to be able to see Gwil's face. I sucked in a choppy breath. "My love, you have so much of what I need—"

"But not everything you need. Be honest," Gwil pleaded, his hands coming up to cup my face, his magic surging through me.

I groaned, unable to lie. "Yes... there is something missing, but we will bond and make it work."

"Fuck! Hold up, bond? What the hell are you talking about? Are you... virgins?" The incredulous expression the man wore morphed into weariness as I nodded, Gwil following suit.

The man's hand fell to his side and he stepped back so fast that I staggered, Gwil grabbing my arm to steady me.

The man lifted his hand as if to ward us off. "This is totally fucked up. You're telling me that you're both novices when it comes to sex?"

I nodded again, relieved that he hadn't picked up on the bonded part.

He rubbed his face, looking back over at Gwil as his stomach grumbled. "When was the last time you both ate something?"

"A few days ago," Gwil answered before I could.

"Shitting hell! Sit down then, before you fall down. And before you ask, no you can't have your clothes back. They stink."

Seeing that the dark look was back on his face, I went over to the table and sat. Gwil quickly followed taking the seat next to mine so that he was facing the man who was still eyeing us like we'd come from some foreign place. Which I suppose Elvedom was, but we had no way of being able to explain it without sounding like we had some sort of mental health disorder. A few days on the streets had revealed quite a few strange folks who'd probably have been better off in an institute.

A rattling sound pulled me from my thoughts as the man moved around his kitchen. It wasn't long before heavenly scents filled the air. The food in Elvedom was mostly plant-based, meat something that was only eaten on occasion. On Earth though, it seemed to be the other way around, not that I was complaining. Given our days with very little food, I'd eat just about anything right now.

I shifted my gaze to Gwil aware that he was more finicky about his food. The need to take care of him that was never too far away coming to the fore as I leaned forward. "Master, can I ask a question?"

"It seems you already have," he said, sighing as he

glanced back over his shoulder at me. "The name is Drake. Master is only used by those who understand what it means and willingly choose to be my submissive." He arched a brow at me as if he was making a point. He licked his lips before speaking again. "What do you want to ask?"

"Gwil has a sensitive stomach and can't eat a lot of things. Can I check what you're giving us?" I asked hesitantly, only releasing the breath I held when the question didn't garner another angry outburst.

"I'm making morning oats. I've got some fresh strawberries; there may be some other fruits in the fridge as well," he offered in a neutral tone, the lines around his eyes deepening as he stared at Gwil.

"I'll be fine with the first two," Gwil replied softly, "Thank you... Daddy."

My breath remained trapped in my lungs as Drake's eyes darkened and his nostrils flared. Oh crap! Had Gwil just pissed him off?

CHAPTER THIRTEEN

Drake

Just get a grip! Come on, keep it together.

No matter how many times I said it to myself, it didn't seem to work. Despite my disbelief at what Gwil had said, my instincts to take care of both men had kicked in. But then Gwil had had to go one further and fuck with my head. Why did Daddy said in that soft voice warm me from head to toe?

I reminded myself that I'd berated Benidic for calling me Master, yet I couldn't find it in me to do the same to Gwil. The selfish part of me wanted to believe that he understood what it meant for him to refer to me in that way. Even though I knew it wasn't true, having been the one to introduce the term to him the previous night when we'd played.

What do you mean, we? You played—they had no say.

I ground my teeth together in an attempt to stop the growl that wanted to break free in response to the truth.

Benidic's shoulders drooped, his head lowering so that his long mane of hair curtained him. It hid his expression from me, the defeated posture doing crazy things to my pulse. I looked away before I did something stupid.

Like everything you've done since meeting these two men hasn't been stupid?

Noticing the oats were about to burn, I took the pan off the stove and then quickly got to work plating the food. Only once everyone had a bowl, did I sit down opposite them. "Eat. Then we're going to have a conversation. If I'm satisfied with your answers, I'll consider what to do next—"

The room filled with Laura Daigle singing *Rescue* from my ring tone, both men jerking and looking around in utter confusion. Their reaction rendered me speechless. The fluttering in my stomach, which seemed ever present with these two turned from butterflies into something more akin to a stampede of horses.

On shaky legs, I went over to the counter to retrieve my phone, Richard's name on the screen. I swiped to answer leaning back against the counter to support myself while keeping an eye on the two men.

"Hey Richard, you're up early this morning. What can I do for you?"

A chuckle came down the line. "The early bird and all that. I hope I didn't disturb you."

"Nah, I'm just about to have breakfast," I replied, nodding at both men to indicate they could eat as neither had touched the food in front of them. There was a hesitation before they picked up the cutlery and delicately picked at their food. Their manners were perfect.

Where had they come from these two? The pieces of the puzzle weren't fitting together right.

"—and so, you see, if you could do that piece first, that would be great," Richard finished.

Shit! What had he asked for first?

"Sorry, what piece do you need?"

"Are you sure I wasn't disturbing you? Has Sonny got your cock in his mouth? Is that what you meant by breakfast?" Richard laughed heartily. I'd been so focused on his offer the previous day that I hadn't brought up the fact that Sonny and I were no longer together.

"Sonny and I, shit, I don't want to talk about it," I bit out.

The two men at the table froze, colour draining from their faces.

What had upset them?

"Sorry, did I just put my foot in it?" Richard sounded distressed, but I was struggling to concentrate on the conversation, the men at the table holding my attention. Gwil placed his knife down and took Benidic's hand in a gesture I was starting to understand as an offer of silent support. Their slender fingers intertwined and, for a moment, I felt bereft at being excluded.

What is wrong with you?

"Listen, if you need time, I can wait for the new sex swing. It's fine."

I shook my head, trying to pull my scattered thoughts together enough to be able to answer Richard. "No, it's fine. If you need the sex swing as a matter of urgency, then I'll work on that." The pair of hands at the table became white-knuckled as I continued to speak.

Finally on track with what Richard was asking for, my brows arched up as I watched the pair's behaviour. From what Richard had said, it would seem that a Dom had got a little too vigorous with the previous leather sex swing, the leather straps ripping. Thankfully, no one had been injured, but it was out of action until I could make another leather seat, straps and a set of stirrups. His request for an additional head restraint, as well as bondage straps stirred my blood, a picture forming in my mind of Benidic strapped to the swing.

"Okay, give me a few days and I'll figure it out." I said goodbye and then turned my phone off, looking over at the two men who still had almost full plates of food in front of them. I tilted my head. "You guys not hungry?"

Both men flushed, Gwil immediately releasing Benidic's hand and starting to eat the fruit and oats. Benidic though, continued to stare at me. "What's on your mind, Benidic?"

His pinched expression didn't alter as he held my gaze. "We could help you... with the... se... making of... the... well, those things you talked about." By the time he'd finished, he was no longer pale his face flushed bright red instead and his top lip sheened with sweat. The silver of his eyes looked like liquid metal and I was sure I could see desire in their depths.

"Do you know anything about working with leather, wood, or metal?" I asked, my voice full of scepticism. For some reason, I got the impression that neither had worked a day in their lives. Benidic shifted uncomfortably on the seat, his lips pinched.

"We have many skills. I'm sure if you direct us, you'll find us very helpful," Gwil answered, his lips curling up as a small smile graced his mouth. There was still uncertainty and what I thought might be sadness in his eyes, but there didn't seem to be any dishonesty. He clearly believed that he would be able to help.

I glanced down at the delicate hands holding the cutlery before lifting my gaze back to his face. "Your hands say differently. They're as smooth as a baby's bottom suggesting that you're not used to manual work."

The air became trapped in my chest at the increasing wattage of Gwil's smile, his whole face brightening.

"Oh Daddy, you don't need to worry about my hands, they're... magical," he smirked, looking smug and confident for the first time since I'd met him.

Gwil appeared unaware of how naturally he'd called me daddy, whereas Benidic seemed only too aware, his head swinging around to stare at a still beaming Gwil. Benidic eventually stopped trying to drill a hole in the side of Gwil's head with his eyes. I got the distinct impression he wasn't used to seeing this side of Gwil.

I walked back over to the table, eyeing the plate of cold food before picking it up and carrying it over to the microwave. I blasted it for thirty seconds before returning to the table. Both men had resumed eating, their gaze fixed on their plates. Their tiny, measured bites reminded me again that there was something not quite right with the picture they were portraying. What was I missing?

My stomach growled as the scent of oats wafted up to me. I pushed the questions aside and chose to eat wolfing down the food without ceremony. After I'd finished, I grabbed three coffees from the counter.

Sat opposite them, I leaned back in my chair sipping the coffee and letting the caffeine do its job of clearing away the dregs of tiredness caused by the lack of sleep. The buzz felt good, even if it did little to expel the anxiety that hadn't shifted from my gut.

I gathered my thoughts, trying to think without my dick or my own needs interfering. "First, I think you need to start by explaining how you came to be in my shop. Then... maybe we can talk about what I'm gonna do with the pair of you."

CHAPTER FOURTEEN

Gwil

I swallowed the mouthful of food that threatened to choke me before laying my cutlery down. I glanced around for something to wipe my lips on, fidgeting when I didn't see anything. Benidic was tense beside me, remaining mute as Drake sat back.

This different side to Benidic was both enlightening and frustrating. I was so used to him speaking for me that now he didn't, I wasn't sure if the new dynamic was good or bad.

Drake continued to sip his coffee, his gaze moving between the two of us. His air of dominance seemed to fill the room making the food in my belly churn.

Benidic's offer to help with the making of... well, whatever it was that Drake was going to make gave us the chance to help him. I'd jumped in with both feet before I'd had a proper opportunity to think about it. His appraisal had been like being dunked in one of the many icy lakes in Elvedom. And then I'd gone and lost my mind. The need to make it right, to show that we could help had taken over, and I'd mentioned magic, nearly exposing myself and Benidic in the process. And if that wasn't bad enough, Daddy had tripped off my tongue like it was the most natural thing in the world.

I hadn't dared to look at Benidic as his gaze had bored a hole in me, concentrating on smiling brightly at Drake in order to distract him from my slip up. Mentioning magical hands was hardly going to keep what we were secret. *Was it?*

Finding no answer, I focused on Drake's lack of faith in our ability. Although he wasn't completely wrong about manual work, our magic could create anything. We just needed to be able to imagine it and with a little trickery, we could make whatever Drake needed.

Thinking about the conversation on the phone had me remembering the device that instead of ringing had sung words. This was still something that caused us surprise because they made so many different noises, Drake again looking at us with suspicion.

Elvedom, given its magic, didn't require some of these human gadgets. And though both Benidic and I were quick learners, it was still hard to adjust. I had questions about the metal box which heated up food in seconds, but I'd managed to suppress them. One of which was why he hadn't used it to cook the food in the first place.

Stop avoiding the one question you want answered. I swallowed a sigh, no longer able to hide from what I wanted to know. Who was Sonny? Was he Drake's chosen mate? Drake's face had shown pain before he'd turned away.

"Are either of you going to talk?" Drake's gaze focused on me and I shoved aside my concern about who Sonny was. "If I recall, you asked me to give Benidic what he wanted in return for explaining yourselves. You wouldn't be going back on that now, would you?" His dark brows rose and although his voice was soft, I didn't miss the thread of steel in it.

The deep-seated need to please this man came to the fore again, taking charge of my tongue. "Three... no four days ago, we were kicked out... onto the streets and well, we're not used to coping on our own. We've been roaming around, hoping to find someone to help to prove that we..." I trailed off, my teeth raking my lower lip.

I glanced sideways at Benidic, praying he'd jump in at any time. But his pursed lips and lowered head said he wasn't going to be any help. Therefore I battled on, unsure whether the partial truth was just digging a bigger hole. "Our parents want us to show that we've grown up and can take responsibility for our actions." That, at least, was the truth, Drake's shoulders relaxing a fraction. I seemed to have done something right.

"Your folks kicked you out with nothing? Not even money?"

I squirmed in my chair as his eyes narrowed on me, but I nodded because it was the truth.

"Was it because you're gay?" he growled.

I shook my head, my hair sliding over my body and teasing my bare skin. I sucked in a breath, hoping to quell the shivers causing goosebumps to spread over my body. "No, being gay wasn't the issue. We were foolish and caused some damage to the pal..." I pulled up short at the near slip up, heat flaring to life and spreading up my neck and my face. *What a fool.* There was no way he'd believe us if I said palace. There was no way we'd have been in the palace in London for Elvedom's sake!

In response to my internal meltdown, Benidic's cool hand landed on top of mine squeezing and giving me some much-needed support. "I'm what my father calls a hellion and I can't seem to keep out of trouble. I wrecked a few rooms in our home by experimenting with some... science projects. Let's just say that when you combine certain elements, it can be disastrous to furniture." He shrugged his slim shoulders, his hair gleaming in the light coming through the window.

"We both did it, Benidic," I muttered, not wanting him to shoulder all the blame. I switched my attention from Benidic to Drake but his face was an unreadable mask.

"And you want me to believe that you won't do anything daft, like blowing up my workshop on a whim?" He leaned on the table as he gave a disparaging laugh, his eyes fierce. "I need to be able to trust those that I work with."

There was something in his gaze that implied that he wasn't just talking about work. My heart skipped a beat.

"What you're telling me means I can't trust either of you. Which also begs the question why you think I need help?"

This time when I squirmed it was because my dick was telling me that it would be more than happy to show Drake just how much he could trust me. Instead of standing up and crawling into his lap like I desperately wanted to do though, I shook off Benidic's hand and hid mine under the table.

"Hands where I can see them, boy," Drake demanded a second later.

Swallowing a sigh at how easily he'd read my intention to touch my throbbing cock, I placed my hands back on the table. "Sorry Daddy." Daddy sounded so right when it slipped out. Calling him that was starting to feel as natural as breathing.

His hand shot across the table. His fingers pinched my

chin, his eyes dark pools that made my body clench in anticipation. "Did you touch your cock?"

I felt the tension gather in the room, Benidic shifting next to me as if he was preparing to do something.

My arse cheeks tightened and I nodded with way too much eagerness. "Yes Daddy," I whispered, compelled to tell the truth.

My chin was released as Drake sat back. I sagged against the chair at a loss to why I felt disappointed that he'd not... not what? Spanked me? A shiver raced through me lodging itself in my groin.

I'd expected something, but a furrowed brow and narrowed gaze wasn't it.

"I can't quite figure out if you're playing me, or if you're both genuinely this naïve." His lips pursed, his hands raking through his jet-black hair. "I need to give this some thought, figure out what I'm going to do." He spoke as if he was talking to himself rather than us.

Yet the urge to push, to convince him that we could help took hold. "Why don't you give us something to do while you're thinking?" I shrugged nonchalantly, praying he couldn't hear the desperation in my voice. "Maybe that way it would help you to work out if we can be useful."

For a few seconds, I thought he was going to refuse, but then the unreadable mask slipped back into place. "Okay. I cut out some leather yesterday. They need to be sewn together to make a leather corset. The pattern should be easy enough to follow if you know what you're doing." One brow rose as if suggesting we didn't, even though he didn't voice it.

"I'm sure both Benidic and I will be able to manage that." I gave a smile that I hoped appeared confident. My hands buzzed with magic, the ball of anxiety twisting my belly relaxing slightly.

It was going to be alright. We'd make the things he needed and then we could go... *home*. Things would go back to the way they used to be before this nightmare started. *That was a good thing, it was.*

Then why didn't it feel good?

CHAPTER FIFTEEN

Drake

The sounds of low voices carried from the room I'd designated for Gwil and Benidic to work in. It was a small storeroom predominantly used to store my supply of leather. I'd chosen it specifically because there were no windows in there, which meant the bright sunlight couldn't fade or dry out the leather. Only thing was, it gave the room a heady scent of new leather. If I spent any time in there the arousal it provoked made it difficult to concentrate. For me, the fragrance was an embodiment of the BDSM world I chose to live in. The smell of leather had been getting stronger with each passing hour the two men spent in the room, along with the scent of arousal.

"Fuck," I muttered, dropping the small hammer I held and lifting my thumb to suck it into my mouth in an effort to ease the throbbing. I'd lost count of how many times I'd hit it. I eyed the piece of metal I'd hammered into... a nondescript shape that didn't even slightly resemble the spider mouth gag I'd been attempting to create. There were no smooth metal loops to attach the leather straps to, to secure it around the head. Nor was there a nice, round gap in the middle for a cock to slip straight into the gaping mouth.

Wisps of arousal tingled through my lower body as images I didn't want in my head, flooded my mind. *Why did you think keeping your distance from the two fuckers would stop your cravings?*

I ignored the nagging thought as I stared at my worktop. The sound of my huffing filled the quiet room as I became increasingly annoyed that my mind wasn't where it was supposed to be, which was on my work. I swung around, stomping over to the corner of the room where my large leather, handmade spanking bench was. The cherry-red corset sitting on top of the padded bench drew my gaze and I picked it up.

The corset was designed to restrain the wearer. Two long straps dangled from both sides. They could be used to bind the arms and legs in various positions, either in front or behind—legs apart and bound around the thigh with arms behind. Or the wearer could be on their stomach with their legs bent and tied to their wrists. There were endless possibilities and, along with my handmade spanking bench, it was one of my favourite things to use. There were multiple options to torment my sub.

As I inhaled, the fragrant scent of new leather filled my nostrils, my groin tightening further. Blood flowed from one head to another as I rubbed my fingers over the fine stitching, trying to distract myself from where my mind wanted to go. The days of seeing, scenting, but not touching either man had been the worst sort of cruelty.

After setting them to work in my leather room on the first day, I'd gone to shower hoping it would help clear my head. I'd made a silent promise that I'd keep my hands to myself until I'd figured out what the pair's game was.

How's that going for you?

It was going fucking nowhere, that's where it was going.

I'd taken their dirty clothes and thrown them in the washing machine. There was no wallet, no keys, no phone, nothing in their pockets to say who they were or where they'd come from.

I'd been forced to consider, yet again, that they might be telling the truth about having been thrown out with nothing.

Maybe they'd hidden their stuff before they broke in just in case they got caught? I didn't think that was the case though as they hadn't tried to leave to go and collect anything. Which begged the question, what had really happened to make their parents throw them out? It seemed a little harsh to kick someone out just for damaging furniture that could easily be replaced.

Even though my own parents were in their seventies, I doubted they would kick me out on the streets if I still lived with them, no matter what I'd done. Fuck, I'd done some pretty heavy-duty shit in the past that had raised a few eyebrows, but they'd never once threatened to toss me out on my ear.

Maybe their parents were a lot stricter? Some of those religious types that liked to insist people paid for their sins? I shook my head. It didn't add up. Nothing in my instincts said that they had past trauma in their lives. They didn't have that beaten-down look about them. The list of things that didn't make sense about them just kept on growing.

Top of the list was the fact that they didn't sound like native Londoners. In fact, I'd been unable to place their accent at all. It was like nothing I'd ever heard before, begging the question of how they'd got to London from wherever it was they came from without any money? Then there was their innocence in contrast to their needy behaviour. If Gwil was to be believed, and my gut was inclined to do exactly that, then they were about as experienced with sex as a young boy only just discovering what his dick was for.

Yeah, it was all one big fucking messy puzzle, which I was no closer to figuring out. As the days passed and they continued to do everything I asked of them, my confusion grew. The upside to it was that my bank balance was no longer looking as scary though.

I stared at the corset, at the tiny handmade stitches and beautiful craftsmanship.

How were they doing it?

After I'd delivered the replacement leather swing, along with the added extras Richard had requested courtesy of Gwil and Benidic's talented hands, my business orders had tripled. After seeing the corset, I'd been so impressed that I'd cut out the black leather needed for the swing and explained to them what I needed. I'd still been a little sceptical, thinking that the corset had probably been a fluke, a one-off thing. I wasn't convinced that they were capable of such fine workmanship, even with the evidence right in front of me. Yet, as I'd busied myself carving wood in my shed for a St Andrew's cross they'd followed my intricate design to the letter, producing a stunning leather swing which felt magical to the touch. I was fucked if I could explain it, but the leather had somehow felt alive.

When I'd gone to Richard's club that night he'd been pleasantly shocked by how fast I'd completed the order. He'd also not been immune to the way the leather felt. Neither it would seem were his clientele, if my overflowing inbox of orders was anything to go by.

Over the last couple of days, I'd cut countless pieces of

leather for my designs and asked them to stitch them. Nothing seemed to phase either man. They'd worked quicker than seemed humanly possible. The evidence was right there on the floor, in the number of completed orders boxed and ready to be sent out.

Each day I awoke thinking it must be a dream, but then I'd hear the sounds above me and reality would hit. Why hadn't they left when I'd gone to the club that night to drop off the goods to Richard? Why had they stayed?

I shook my head, my fingers tightening on the soft leather of the corset I still held. A corset that I'd initially planned to sell, but now...

No, you swore to yourself that there'd be no more touching until you have all the answers.

I lifted my gaze to the open door, the ache in my lower back reminding me of where I'd slept the last few nights. Although the sofa was massive and very comfy, it wasn't meant to be slept on for three nights straight.

Then stop pissing about and go and claim what you want.

The voice, which wasn't my own, had become so familiar over the last few days that I no longer jerked at hearing it.

"Shut up. I've told you I'm not listening." The petulance in my voice was enough to make me hunch over. The ridiculousness of talking to no one wasn't lost on me, but I was at a loss at how to change it.

You know what you need to do to change it.

This time I growled loudly, dropping the corset back on the bench. I stalked over to the other side of the room and picked up the hammer, eyeing the clutter in front of me as I did so. I groaned at the mess, my father's voice running through my head and reminding me to tidy up after myself.

My hands automatically reached for the tools, hanging them back on the hooks on the wall.

After my father's retirement ten years earlier, my parents had moved to Brighton. I'd opted to sell my apartment, move into the building and turn it into my home, as well as my business. I'd spent quite a bit of money updating the large, three-storey building. The top floor was full of many generations worth of junk, or treasures depending upon how it was viewed. My father hadn't parted with much over the years and neither had Grandpa. That meant that the top floor had been a daunting prospect to empty when I'd taken over ownership. So I'd pretended it didn't really exist, only going up there if I had something I needed to store, or if I was checking the roof. The winters in London were bleak and the damage from heavy rainfall, if left unchecked could lead to problems.

But not even at my lowest ebb had I ever considered selling the property. In today's market, being just off Regents Park, it was worth a fortune. My great grandpa had purchased the place decades ago during a recession, envisaging that it might be worth more in the future. He'd been a canny old bugger like that. The house my parents had moved into had also been one of his purchases. The shoe-making business had been profitable back then, the skills required passed down the generations, first to his son, then to my father and then finally to me.

Look at what you've done with it!

My eyes ached as tears welled up. I'd not told my father how bad things had got over the past few months. The idea of explaining that I'd fucked up made my stomach drop and my heart pound.

I was a failure. Even given all the past generations' hardships, they'd not fucked up as badly as I had. The sound of grinding teeth filled the room as I thought about all the money I'd wasted over the last two years on Sonny. Money I could have used to help keep the business afloat.

My vision blurred and tears slid down my face, chilling it in the warm room.

Get a grip. Your luck is changing, think of all the orders you have!

Yeah, but what if... what if Gwil and Benidic left? Where would that leave me?

Right back where you started, alone!

Panic gripped my throat and the air refused to budge from my lungs. I wasn't worried about the business, but at the prospect of not seeing them daily.

You're being ridiculous! These men have been in your home for mere days.

What did it matter if they left? I'd spent years making the business work. I could do it again. I could. They'd leave and things would carry on as normal.

That's what you think, came the sly voice.

Fucking hell!

CHAPTER SIXTEEN

Benidic

I lifted my hands, checking the open doorway before allowing my magic to pulse, the orbs of red light spreading out over the large piece of burgundy leather in front of me. Gwil moaned quietly, shifting next to me. The scent of his arousal mixed with the intoxicating aroma of leather.

I resisted looking at him as my hands warmed and the leather became the garment Drake had designed and cut out. Once I was happy that the stitches were perfect, and that everything matched the picture in front of me, I lay the completed item to one side. Getting up off the chair, I squeezed past Gwil, my naked skin rubbing all too briefly against his. There was a sharp inhale, Gwil's body quivering as his hands fluttered above the piece of leather he was working on, but he didn't look at me.

Drake had refused to give us back our clothes, so we'd stayed naked. Not that he took much notice. I swallowed a sigh and ignoring my stiff cock, went over to the wall of shelves in front of the small table we'd spent days working at. The cock cage had long since been removed, a part of me wishing that Drake would put it back on. It would help with the constant feeling of being on edge, my arousal unrelenting.

Focusing on what I needed to do next, as much as I was able to anyway, I stepped closer to the wall. The room was small, but had been designed to maximize the space available. The wall in front of me had shelving from floor to ceiling, deep enough to hold the large rolls of leather. On the lower shelves there were multiple boxes labelled with things from threads, to buckles, to odd bits of metal that made no sense to me or Gwil, but we were sure had their purpose.

Everything was in order, demonstrating an organised person had set it up. It had made finding what we needed easier, not that we actually needed any of it. Our magic could have created each piece solely from the pictures Drake had drawn, but as Gwil had pointed out it would look suspicious if we didn't use anything.

Gwil, who was always the sensible one, explained that we needed to get into Drake's good graces, to avoid making him any more wary than he already was. I'd got so caught up in how to please Drake with my magic that I hadn't considered the ramifications. *No*, I'd been so wrapped up in his *pleasure* that I'd not considered the fact that by doing what he wanted, he'd no longer do any of the things we'd done together on the first night.

As the days wore on, I started to kick myself, my dick supercharged with unrelenting arousal. Being naughty definitely held more appeal after a taste of the forbidden. This being good lark had garnered me what? *Nothing, that's what.*

I'd been going around and around in circles and each time it led back to the same dilemma. How did I get more attention from Drake? Each idea I had only made it harder to control my dick. It leaked copious amounts of pre-cum against my bare thighs, showing anyone who chose to look exactly where my mind was. Not that either Gwil or Drake were paying attention.

Even though he was in no better state than I was, Gwil refused to let me do anything about it when we were alone in bed together. On the first night that Drake had left us alone and gone to sleep on the couch, Gwil had cried himself to sleep, refusing to talk to me for the first time I could remember.

It cut at my heart, making it throb like an open wound. At a loss as to how to fix it, I'd given him space, hoping he'd forgive me as he usually did. Unfortunately, I was still waiting for that to happen and although he was naturally drawn to me when he slept, he remained just as aloof when he was awake.

When he lay plastered all over me in the mornings, his dick hard and leaking, he remained adamant that nothing would happen between us without Drake. Secretly, I was thrilled at the thought of the three of us together. Gwil obviously understood that Drake wouldn't take anything from our relationship, but that instead he would provide the missing piece that we both needed to make us fit.

A part of me felt like Drake also felt the connection between us, especially when he'd given us access to books and a computer and directed us to BDSM sites for research. It had given us the answers to all the questions we'd asked that first night. Gwil fitted right into being a boy and as for me, dear Elvedom, I wanted to be his submissive. I wanted him to be my master, to control me, to punish me in the way that I craved deep inside.

The only thing was, knowing that didn't help me to figure out how to get what I wanted, or give me the much-needed release that my oversensitive dick begged for. I knew I could do it myself in the bathroom if I wanted to. But I didn't want that. I wanted Drake and Gwil to control my pleasure. Therefore, I was left in hell with the added stimulation from the scent of leather and Gwil's own arousal teasing me mercilessly. I was at the end of my tether. I really was.

How in the hell did I get more of what I'd done with Drake and Gwil on the first night?

The sound of laboured breathing came from the table as I stretched up to grab the cut pieces of leather. I squeezed my arse several times, making sure to display my body before turning to face the red-faced man sat at the table. Gwil's gaze was fixed hungrily on the dick jutting out from my body, the tip glistening under the ceiling lights.

My heart thundered in my ears, a pearly drop appearing on the tip of my dick as Gwil's tongue slid over his lower lip. For days, I'd endured this erotic torture. If it had been my father's mission to make me suffer, then he'd succeeded. The torment was like none I'd ever experienced before and it was a total mind fuck.

Had my father known that the sexual bonds binding us would break? No, that was ridiculous. If Father had had any idea what he'd done when he'd sent us here, I was sure he'd have had us back in Elvedom in a split second. There was no way he'd be happy with the removal of the bonds placed on us by the council.

"Suck my dick," I begged, not caring whether Drake heard me. I needed something, anything, to relieve the tension gripping me by the balls—literally. It had been five days since I'd felt Gwil's mouth on my cock and I wanted it. No, I needed it.

His violet eyes turned a deep shade of purple and his

skin glowed, but he shook his head. "Daddy wouldn't like it—"

"How do you know? You haven't asked him. And if he wanted to be your Daddy, then why is he keeping his distance from *both* of us?" I stressed the both, hoping that it would make him do as I'd pleaded.

His face fell, tears sliding down his now ashen face.

"Oh fuck, I'm sorry," I cried, dropping the leather bundle I held and skipping around the table with the intention of taking him in my arms.

I'd gone no more than a few steps though when I heard a noise. The air became stuck somewhere between my chest and throat as I looked towards the door and met Drake's stormy gaze.

"What's going on in here?" he ground out through a clenched jaw, his hands on his hips and his foot tapping on the wooden floor.

"He was being mean. Benidic says you don't want to be my Daddy," Gwil said, sobbing. He buried his head in his hands, his long, dark hair falling forwards and covering the piece of leather he'd been working on.

The sound broke my heart, but the selfish part of me wondered whether this would be enough trouble to get more of what Drake dished out in his special room. As if he'd read my mind, he stalked over to me, his fingers cupping the back of my head in a punishing hold. His gaze met mine and my cock bucked in excitement. *Holy Elvedom!*

"Are you being naughty on purpose, sub?"

The smooth voice with the dark edge to it sent a shiver through me and all I could do was nod.

His eyes narrowed, but then his face became unreadable as his gaze shifted over to Gwil. "Come here to Daddy."

It wasn't a question and Gwil didn't hesitate for a second. He moved so fast that I had to bite my lip to stop a smile from appearing.

Drake's other arm lifted so that Gwil could tuck himself against his chest. The sadness that had hung over him like a dark cloud dissipated the moment that Drake hugged him into his divine-smelling body. A body that smelt of wood and leather combined with Drake's musky scent. I swallowed a moan of approval, not sure whether it would help or hinder my cause.

At the sound of raised voices, I'd dropped the wooden humbler and the piece of sandpaper I'd been using on it. My heart rate triple-timed as I ran down the hall to see what the commotion was all about.

Once I was in the room the tension had buzzed like an electric saw. Fuck, it had fried whatever remaining brain cells I'd had left after the pair had already taunted and teased me to the point of madness.

It was your idea to leave them naked.

Shutting out the voice of reason, I wrapped my arm around Gwil's naked back. In a moment of weakness and needing to comfort my boy, I buried my face in his sweet-smelling hair.

He is not your boy.

He's not my boy, yet!

He melted against me, his hard arousal pushing against my hip. The loose, cotton shorts I wore did little to prevent the firmness of his dick from branding my flesh.

The charged air made it impossible to take a decent

breath, my chest heaving. Sweat slid down my back, my hand clenching on Benidic's nape, the feel of silky hair against my palm only adding to my torment. I inhaled and my nose filled with the scent of leather, two very sweet-smelling men and pre-cum. It was a heady mix, one I wanted to wallow in all fucking day.

Gwil, seemingly unaware of the tension riding me, rubbed against me purring like a kitten. Benidic's neck strained in my grip and I lifted my head to meet his defiant, silvery eyes.

My efforts of the last few days to valiantly ignore what was going on had come back to bite me in the arse. I'd seen the perfect storm of sexual tension building between the two of them during their heated exchanges. *And it had built in me too.*

Had I done this on purpose to test them? To test myself? Had I kept them naked so I could see what they'd do to each other without me there?

They've waited for you, said the sly voice. A voice that had become increasingly persistent over the last two days. To the point where I'd struggled to determine whether I was just projecting another voice in an attempt to deflect from what I wanted to do, or whether I was going mad. It was a close call, neither prospect filling me with joy.

I sighed, knowing that no matter how much I tried to persuade myself that I'd wanted to avoid this, it was useless. It had been heading this way ever since I hadn't kicked their pert backsides out of the door. I'd made them comfortable in my home and in my bed. I'd even given them the means to research my lifestyle which had kept them quiet for hours before they'd scurried to bed, the whispered arguments starting again once they got there.

It was about time I dropped the pretence about what was going to happen. This was going to end in... in what? *Everything you've ever dreamed of. Everything.*

The word did little to help the control that I was slowly losing my grip on. *You're forty fucking six and a Dom, own your shit.*

Feeling more rattled than I wanted to admit, I stood taller and took several deep breaths. The moment felt monumental as I closed my eyes to shut both men out, giving myself a minute.

Was I going to do this again? Was I really going to take away their choice? *They have more information this time. Do they? Do they really get what this all means to me?*

Benidic's body jerked, a deep moan rumbling through his chest as his eyes opened. All the unanswered questions flew right out of my head. Because who wanted answers when they were faced with a gloriously naked man teasing his purple-headed cock which was leaking like a broken faucet?

His eyes dared me to stop him. Every muscle in my body strained with the need to teach him who the Master was. The dominance I normally tamped down on flowed like lava out of a volcano, demolishing any good intentions which stood in its path. Acknowledging the feelings, I took a deep inhale and embraced that side of myself.

"Gwil, Daddy needs to let go so he can teach Benidic a lesson, okay?" I nuzzled the top of Gwil's head gently before releasing him. He trembled, but there was nothing but excitement on his glowing face.

He gave a meek nod, his gaze shifting to Benidic in my arms before giving a smug grin. "Daddy's going to teach you a lesson and I'm going to help."

He glanced back at me as he said the last part and I couldn't stop the evil grin which spread across my face. "I'm sure I can find my boy something to do." I left the words hanging there, letting both men's imagination do their worst.

I tightened my grip on Benidic. "Did I say you could touch your dick? Did I say you could pleasure yourself?" I rasped out, deliberately deepening my voice to reaffirm that I was in charge, not him. He hesitated, his hand still on his dick, but then he let go.

I released the breath I wasn't even aware I'd been holding while waiting to see if he'd play along. My heart swelled as he lowered his gaze, his hands clasped at his lower back. It looked slightly awkward though, given my firm hold on his neck.

"Are you trying to be a good sub, hmm?" I swallowed a chuckle as his eyelashes fluttered, but he didn't shift his gaze to mine. I moved my mouth to his ear to whisper, "We both know you're not." He shivered, goosebumps spreading over his skin, his pale pink nipples budding.

Without releasing Benidic, I turned to Gwil. "Sweet baby, go into my work room. On the bench is a piece of wood that I've been working on. Will you bring them to the playroom?" There was no hesitation to his nod as he spun on his heel, his raven tresses shining like polished glass under the lights. It swirled around his willowy frame as he hurried to get what I'd asked. I returned my attention to Benidic, recalling that with more time than I'd known what to do with, I'd tidied up the playroom so there were no small pieces of leather lying around that I could use.

I shouted after Gwil. "Can you find me a small piece of leather as well?"

"Yes, Daddy," came Gwil's reply from somewhere down the hall.

Happy that he'd do as I'd asked, I gave Benidic a devilish smile. "Are you ready?"

His chest rose rapidly, but his head moved in agreement as much as it could within the confines of my hand. "Good, because today you're going to learn a valuable lesson about not pissing off our sweet baby, or your Master."

I deepened my voice, projecting a little more menace than usual just to see how he'd react. I wasn't disappointed, his dick bucking hard and his whole body freezing. My gaze swept over his body stopping at the sac containing his balls which had ridden so close to his body that I could barely see it. Unable to resist the temptation to torment him further, I swirled my fingertip in the pre-cum slicking the head of his dick and spreading it over the head in lazy circles. His eyes became hooded and he was boneless as he melted under my firm grip. I could have sworn that my hand was the only thing still holding him up.

"Ohhhhh, nooooo," he groaned. He stilled, his mouth hanging open as I pushed my nail into his slit. His gaze shifted to mine as I kept up the pressure. Wide eyes begged for more and I gave him what he wanted, for now anyway. Increasing the pressure, I dug my nail in hard.

"Oh... oh... Gods... oh... yes... pleaseeeeeee," he moaned in a breathless, whispery voice that made my dick harder than steel. I pushed aside my own need though as it tried to drill a hole in my shorts, continuing to drive Benidic wild instead.

The tension riding his willowy body prevented him from hiding what was about to happen. He shrieked in protest as I withdrew my finger and quickly squeezed his sac, hard enough to stop him from coming. He glowered at me, but I just shrugged, completely unrepentant.

One of his brows rose, but I eyed him until his gaze lowered reluctantly.

Gods, he was going to be so much fun.

CHAPTER EIGHTEEN

Gwil

At the sound of Benidic's cry, I clutched the piece of wood and leather in my hand, rushing from the workroom, down the long passageway and into the playroom, only to find it empty. I ran back down the hallway towards the room we'd been working in, my dick bouncing joyfully.

Although my heart was doing a dance in my chest, it was all from excitement. From the moment Drake had acknowledged that I was indeed his boy, I'd been in seventh heaven. The hurt that had wanted to take hold firmly pushed aside with the anticipation of what might follow. I wasn't stupid and neither was Drake. He had to be aware of the game Benidic was playing. He'd clearly been trying to goad us to get what he wanted.

My steps slowed.

What did Drake really want? Someone to play with but then toss aside once he'd had enough? The internet might be full of information, but a lot of it was confusing. And if I was honest, I'd got stuck on the sites that were mainly about

Daddy kink. They'd given me insight into why I loved it when both Benidic and Drake took care of me. It would seem I was a submissive, but not in the same way Benidic craved.

No, I didn't want to be whipped, or chained, or any of those other things. A shiver raced down my spine and my arse tingled. Heat rose up my chest and neck as I remembered the spanking Drake had given Benidic. Okay, maybe I wanted a spanking, but the other stuff? Yeah, Benidic could keep that for himself.

I hesitated at the doorway, a wave of intense desire sweeping through me at the stunning picture Drake and Benidic made together. Drake held Benidic by the neck and his balls, Drake's expression dark and moody. Benidic's eyes were lowered, but his body screamed defiance as if he was taunting Drake to do his worst.

A flash of emotion left me breathless. *Were these men really mine or was this only a game?*

Once the thought took hold, a flood of uncertainties came with it. My hands became clammy at the memory of the conversation Drake had had on the phone, along with what I'd found in the wardrobe in his bedroom.

Had Sonny been Drake's boy? His sub?

I clutched the leather and wood to my chest as I tried to ward off the questions.

Did all the clothes in the wardrobe belong to Sonny? Ever since I'd not been able to resist the temptation to open the wardrobe in Drake's room, only to find it full of clothes that clearly weren't his, I'd been asking myself the same question.

I'd added two and two together and come up with a number I didn't like. The odd tension between myself and Benidic had made it difficult though to talk about what had been bothering me. My arousal flagged as the unanswered questions crowded my mind.

In my distraction, I automatically stepped closer to both men needing their reassurance. Tears fell unheeded down my cheeks as sobs choked me.

"What, what is it?" Drake ground out, his tone harsher than usual and sounding more than a little panicked.

"Is... is... this... a game?" I asked through my sobs, dropping the things I held so that I could bury my head in my hands and avoid seeing Drake's reaction.

"Let me go," Benidic squealed.

"Hold still, Benidic. Gwil look at me."

It was a command so there was no way I could deny him, not when my heart ached to do as he asked. I lifted my face but found that I couldn't meet his gaze, staring at his dark, stubbly chin instead.

"I won't ask again. Look at me!" he growled.

I slowly inched my gaze upwards until I met his stormy gaze. There was so much emotion in the depths of his eyes that I struggled to breathe. The air in my lungs suddenly felt like the syrup Benidic loved to pour over his pancakes.

"What brought this on? A few minutes ago you were acting like a giddy child. Now you look as if I stole your favourite toy from you." His brow furrowed and his mouth pinched into a straight line.

Clasping my hands together to stop myself from lowering my eyes, I repeated my question. "Is this a game?"

For a second, something flitted across his face. My pulse jumped but the emotion was gone before I could work out what it had meant.

"No, this is not a game to me."

Although, the answer should have made me jump for

joy there was too much reluctance in his confession. I held my breath waiting for him to continue.

"I've known what I've wanted for years." He inclined his head towards me and then looked over at Benidic, who seemed frozen in place. "The way I'm wired means that I need both a sub and a boy. I've tried to do that with one man, but it didn't work for me. In the past, I've... struggled with finding a pair of men who were willing to share the way I needed..." His dark brows met in the middle as he trailed off.

Were we in the past? *He'd said the past, not the present.*

I scratched the back of my head, tugging on the long strands of my hair. *Just ask him for Elvedom's sake.*

"Are we the present?" I blurted out.

A look of confusion was followed by the twitching of his lips. "Yes, you're the present," he answered, his voice full of amusement. "Have you finished worrying or does Daddy need to explain anything else? Because now is the time to ask."

His gaze moved between Benidic and me, and it was only then that I noticed that he still had hold of Benidic's sac. The bluish tinge to Benidic's sac made my thighs squeeze together. It had to be painful. But Benidic's leaking cock said that it didn't bother him.

Why would it bother him? He's a pain slut, remember.

Giving myself a mental slap, I tried to focus on what Drake had asked.

Did I have anything else I wanted explained?

"Who is Sonny?" My hand covered my mouth at the sour expression which pinched Drake's lips together.

Benidic whined, giving me an angry glare as Drake removed his hands and stepped back from him. I ignored him, focusing on Drake as he came over and took hold of my forearms. There was sadness, anger and what I thought might be regret in his eyes as he stared at me.

"Sonny was my sub and my boyfriend for a couple of years. He left me a... couple of weeks ago. It would seem that he was more interested in my bank balance than he was in me. Now it's not as full, he's moved on to pastures new." His powerful shoulders shrugged as if he didn't care, but he hadn't managed to mask the underlying hurt in his voice.

In tune with me, Benidic came up behind Drake, wrapping his arms around his waist as I stepped closer and tugged my arms free from Drake's grasp to wrap them around both men. Drake stiffened for a second, my stomach clenching at the thought that he might reject us. But then there was a long, heartfelt sigh, his stiff posture relaxing as he took the comfort we were offering. The silence lengthened but it wasn't uncomfortable.

I stroked the warm, silky skin of Benidic's naked back as Drake lowered his chin to rest it on top of my head. His arms tightened around me, his breath evening out. The sexual tension that never seemed too far away when we were all together, abated, as the moment stretched and we just enjoyed the simple pleasure of holding each other.

CHAPTER NINETEEN

Drake

The lingering hurt and betrayal I'd felt towards Sonny couldn't be sustained, not with the waves of affection coming from Benidic and Gwil wrapped around me. Their simple gesture of support, of acceptance, left me struggling to contain the well of emotions that I was starting to recognise was stronger than anything I'd ever felt for Sonny. In fact, stronger than for anyone I'd ever dated before.

What the fuck was happening? God knows! But as my arms tightened around Gwil and I rested my chin on his head with the heat of Benidic against my back, my heart swelled with joy. As I Inhaled the scent of Gwil's hair, my breaths evened out, the tension surrounding us disappearing. I knew it wouldn't last long, but the moment was as perfect as it could get.

I prayed that this wasn't some huge cosmic joke where I was going to find myself knocked back on my arse, unable to get up again.

Stop it. Accept it for what it is. You can't control everything!

The thought disappeared as Benidic chose that moment to push his aroused dick between my thighs. It would seem that he was ready to play. My gaze landed on the wooden humbler that Gwil had dropped when he'd got upset. If either man had seen the smile spreading across my face, I was sure that they would have run for the hills. I struggled to get my lips back into a straight line as I eased out of their hold.

I looked back over my shoulder at Benidic. "Are you trying to push me?" I raised one brow, a flush lighting up his face as his gaze shifted to the floor. I swallowed a chuckle at his lack of contrition. Turning to Gwil, I gave him a sly wink, inclining my head towards the humbler. "Bring that to Daddy, please."

He scrubbed at his cheeks as if ridding himself of any remaining tears before giving me an endearing smile that would have melted the most hardened heart. Mine fluttered madly in my chest and I prayed that there wasn't a sappy look on my face. Gwil's smile increased though and the hope died.

Before I could say anything more, he swung around, bending gracefully at the waist to flash his pert ass at me as he picked up the humbler. His slim muscular legs seemed endlessly long and his almost translucent skin gleamed in the overhead light. Blood swiftly pooled in my groin, a wave of dizziness sweeping through me. I took a deep, steadying breath, closing my eyes for a second to try and prevent myself from pouncing on him and ravishing that tight, pale arse.

"Daddy, are you okay?" Gwil's sweet concern had my eyelids lifting.

"Yes, sweet boy," I took the humbler from him leaning forward to whisper in his ear. "Daddy just needed a moment to stop himself from pushing his cock deep into your tight little pucker."

"Oh... oh," he gasped, his face flushing bright red and his hands moving restlessly at his sides as if he had no idea what to do with them. His cock, on the other hand, had no problem demonstrating how much it wanted that. Mere seconds ago, it had only been semi-erect but now it was fully aroused.

I couldn't resist teasing him further, my fingertip sliding over the silky head of his dick and giving it a gentle stroke from tip to base. His mouth opened into a perfect "o" and he whimpered, his lower body undulating as I removed my hand.

His heavy-lidded, violet eyes begged me not to stop. "Don't worry, sweet baby. Daddy is going to give you every-thing you need. But first, I need to get my naughty sub prop-erly situated." Gwil's face lit up and he nodded, his gaze moving over to Benidic.

I turned to face Benidic, holding up the humbler. "Do you know what this is? No? Well I'm going to show you." As he shook his head, my heart skipped several beats and I gave him a devilish grin. "Let's take this to my playroom so we can get you... positioned." Benidic's face lost a little of its colour as I paused, but my heart swelled as he stood a little straighter.

I led both men into my playroom, my gaze sweeping the room. After my parents had moved out, I'd decided on this room as being the perfect playroom because it was at the back of the building and had lots of light. The room was large and square with a high ceiling, and big enough to house some of the largest furniture. I'd rigged my hand-crafted St Andrew's cross on a pulley system which suspended it from the ceiling. This allowed me to move it into the middle of the room when it was needed and then push it back against the wall when I wanted to use something else.

The sex swing was my own design as well, as was the spanking bench which had some niffy adaptions to keep things interesting. I also had a leather sofa which could easily fit three people. It sat next to the window which overlooked my work shed. Dark red and black blackout blinds covered the window, matching the furniture. The walls were cream, apart from the wall that housed my collection of bondage gear. That one was painted a dark red colour.

My gaze landed on the wooden chests which housed all sorts of goodies. This time I let the smile spread across my face. Fuck, I couldn't wait to push Benidic to find out where his limits were. With that in mind, I directed Gwil over to sit on the leather seat and then guided Benidic over to the middle of the room. I inhaled and exhaled slowly, hoping it would help to keep my excitement under control.

"Sub, kneel for me," I crooned softly. Benidic lowered himself to the floor without hesitation, his palms resting on his thighs as his head lowered, his hair falling in a silky swathe around his slim shoulders. At the breath-taking sight of him kneeling in the middle of the room, the air caught at the back of my throat. His silver hair and pale body gleamed like a bright diamond nestled in a box of red and black velvet. Only there was no velvet, just leather and wood.

I glanced down at my shorts, my teeth clenching. The ache in my balls and in my dick was far too distracting, and for the first time in my life I wondered if I was going to be able to keep the control I needed. *You can. You can give him what he needs. What you both need.*

My fingers tightened around the humbler as I tensed and relaxed the muscles of my body before crouching next to Benidic. My fingers brushed at the soft, scented strands of his hair uncovering his face. "Did you read about safe words?"

His body shuddered. "Yes," he whispered.

"Good. You'll need three different words. One to tell me you're okay, one to ask for me to slow down and one that will make me stop. They need to be something you don't use all the time, so I know that you mean it when you say it. There can't be any miscommunication between us. Do you understand?"

Another nod and a "yes," this one accompanied by a shaky exhale, but his eyes gleamed with nothing but excitement. He licked his lips. "I'm going to use raven for stop, blondie for I'm okay and..." he trailed off, his gaze moving from mine to look around the room. He smirked, the silver of his eyes turning to gunmetal grey. "Whip for when I want you to slow down." His cocky tone did stupid things to me and I barely resisted the urge to roll my eyes at his over-confidence.

I didn't respond, concentrating on giving the humbler a quick check to ensure that the wood was smooth and silky. I was sure he wouldn't be happy having splinters of wood anywhere near his balls. I ran my hands over the wood twice before laying a hand on his back. "Come up a little and bend forward. Yes, that's it." His body quivered as he did as I'd asked and I placed the curved wood against the back of his thighs.

Reaching between his spread thighs from the back, I carefully cupped his balls in my palm, fondling them gently until Benidic was releasing a steady stream of needy moans and whimpers.

The sound of a moan from where Gwil was sitting caused me to look over in his direction. I faltered for a moment at the sight of the desire swirling in the depths of his now deep purple eyes. His chest was heaving and his knuckles were white from how tightly he had his hands clenched on his bare thighs. It was as if he was trying to resist touching his leaking dick.

"You're being such a good sweet baby for Daddy. I promise you'll be rewarded very soon." My heart flipped over in my chest as his gaze moved to mine.

"I'm trying so hard to be good, Daddy," he whined, his hands fidgeting on his thighs. "But please could you hurry?"

Despite the desperation in his voice, I turned my attention back to Benidic, who had remained still. Not wanting to delay any further, I slipped his balls through the small gap between the two pieces of wood made specially to house a scrotum. With quick efficiency, I secured the two bolts at either end of the wood ensuring it was snug against the back of his legs. His balls were trapped, sat flush against the wood.

"Sit forward." I waited a beat and wasn't disappointed when Benidic let out a loud cry, the movement pushing the wood hard against the back of his legs and stretching the skin of his scrotum painfully.

"Oooohhhhh! Whattt theeee fuckkkkkkk."

I chuckled as he panted, doing his best to remain still so that the humbler didn't tug at what were now presumably aching balls.

"How do you like my humbler? It teaches naughty subs like you, that there's only one master here." Benidic's eyelashes fluttered madly, but he didn't raise his gaze to mine. It took a minute for his breathing to calm down, his body gleaming with sweat. I watched him closely waiting until he'd found a place inside himself that helped him to cope with the pain before I wrapped my hand around his dick and stroked firmly.

His eyes widened, his mouth opening as if he wanted to say something. But instead of speaking, he screamed, his hips jerking forward as I stroked his dick from tip to base. The rough calluses on my palm rubbed at the velvety skin of his cock as I worked my hand up and down it. His entire body juddered and his cries continued to fill the room, his cock showing how much his body craved it as it leaked over my hand and dripped down between his thighs.

Gwil's face was flushed as he leaned forward as if he wanted to get closer. I didn't pause from my movements. "Come here, sweet baby." I hadn't even finished speaking before Gwil was up and off the seat. He all but skidded to a stop in front of me, his cock in no better state than Benidic's as it pointed skyward. The slit was wet and slick, my mouth watering for a taste. My intention had been to get Gwil to suck Benidic's cock but instead I encouraged him closer to me.

"Stand next to Daddy and hold your cock so that I can suck it and Benidic can watch."

CHAPTER TWENTY

Benidic

I thought my mind was going to explode, along with my balls. The pain was unbelievable, like nothing I'd ever experienced before. It was all-consuming, as if it was taking greedy gulps of me, giving me no time to gather my thoughts or to prepare for the next wave of agony.

Yet, the part of me that had always known that there was something missing from my life embraced it like a long-lost lover. I'd felt moments of floaty bliss tied to the pillory, but there something had held me back from letting go completely. This though, fuck, this left me with no place to hide. I felt exposed, every one of my kinky arse needs on display.

When Drake had called to Gwil, my ears had buzzed with the anticipation of what other torture he might make me endure. The pressure from the wood behind my thighs increased, but then released slightly as Drake's hand stopped its heavenly strokes. His actions had made my cock ache and my balls pray for mercy, the skin of my scrotum stretched tighter than a piece of elastic every time I jerked.

I gasped, sucking in greedy gulps of air. My hair was

stuck to my body and face as I tried to keep as still as possible. The evil smile that had been on Drake's face when he'd asked if I knew what he was about to use on me made perfect sense now. The humbler was aptly named, the frantic fluttering in my chest clueing me in to the fact that Drake had only just got started.

"Stand next to Daddy and hold your cock so I can suck it and Benidic can watch."

My groan was heartfelt as I raised my gaze a fraction to watch Gwil do as he'd been bid. His dick looked painfully hard, the head an angry red colour and slick with pre-cum. I licked my lips in anticipation of what was coming. This was the first time Drake was going to do more than touch and my own dick wanted some of that attention, even when I knew what would come with it.

"Please, me too... Master, I'll be good," I begged, but it was to no avail.

Drake gave me a toothy grin. His eyes were alight with devilish amusement and a dark desire that made my balls ache along with my dick. His attention moved back to Gwil as he opened his mouth. Gwil needed no further prompting, sliding his slim cock into the waiting mouth.

Gwil's mouth hung open, Drake's cheeks hollowing as he sucked the whole of his dick into his mouth. When Drake's lips reached the base of Gwil's dick, I cried out. My hips moved forward desperately in need of the same attention, only all I got was excruciating pain. Sweat dripped into my eyes as I struggled not to react to what was happening right in front of my face. I willed my eyes to close, but the fuckers wouldn't obey me, glued as they were to both men. Gwil sounded delirious as he moaned and whimpered, making nonsensical noises as Drake kept his hooded gaze on me the entire time, ramping up my need.

It became a vicious circle. The longer I watched, the harder it was to keep still and the more pain I caused myself. The fact I was inflicting the pain on myself messed with my head, despite knowing that I couldn't really stop it even if I wanted to. My head and body though, seemed to have lost their connection.

A familiar voice chimed in. *No, it's not that. It's that you want this. Stop fighting yourself and embrace what you need.*

"Raven, raven!" I cried out in confusion. The air in my lungs refused to budge, my father's voice still ringing in my head. *Elvedom, he's seen me. He's seen me like this.*

Tears rolled down my cheeks, the heat that had been there moments ago draining away. I frantically searched the room. But as I tried to stand, the pain became all-consuming making it impossible to focus on anything else as black spots obscured my vision. As I fought, Drake's concerned voice cut through the layers of agony.

"What the fuck! Hold still, Benidic! Hold still! Fuck, do as I say!"

When strong arms wrapped around my body, I let go, collapsing against his solid chest as I sobbed uncontrollably. I hid my face in his neck, trying to hide from the knowledge that my father had seen me like this.

There is no place to hide, Benidic!

Sweet Elvedom!

The sound of soft music filtered past the layers of sleep and I snuggled deeper under the covers. I reached out for Gwil but found only a cold spot next to me. I blinked several times to clear the sleep from my eyes. The lamp next to the bed glowed, illuminating the room. But even before I'd looked around, I'd sensed I was alone.

Where was Gwil?

I glanced at the closed curtains, struggling to calculate what time of day it was. As my brain fought past the cloud of cotton wool in an attempt to get back online, the ache I'd not fully registered between my thighs became more prominent. I slid my hands beneath the cover to take hold of what were now very tender, very swollen balls, fondling them carefully. They felt double the size and bruised. *Oh crap!*

Had I done that when I'd panicked? I groaned, turning my head to bury my face in the pillow. The heat in my cheeks increased as the memory of what had caused me to use my safe word returned with a vengeance. My heart rattled against my ribs hard enough that it took some effort to draw in a breath deep enough to fill my lungs.

As the memories flooded my mind, I rolled onto my back, unable to hide any longer from what had happened. Had my father really been talking to me? Telling me to embrace...

I shook my head, unable to finish the thought. It was inconceivable that he could know what I wanted when I hardly even knew myself. It had to have been the pain confusing me. That was all it was, right? I huffed and covered my eyes with my forearm, trying to evade the obvious truth as my heart continued to thunder in my ears.

Son, you can't hide from what you are!

I sat bolt upright, searching the room, ignoring the ache that accompanied the sudden movement. "Show yourself," I cried.

It took a few seconds but then, there my father stood in Drake's bedroom. His colourful, flowing silk robe swirled around his slender frame as he walked over to the bed to stare down at me. His face was easy to read and I cringed. How did he know these things about me?

"Because you are my son *in every way*," he responded to my silent question.

"What do you mean 'in every way?' Am I supposed to understand that?" I hissed through clenched teeth.

His silver brows rose so far up his forehead that I feared they'd disappear into his hairline. But it was his head tilting to one side in a gesture I was more than familiar with that had me apologising. "I'm sorry, Father. But this," I lifted my arms, but let them flop back down when I couldn't sum up what "this" was. "I don't know what all this is. Now you're in the human realm, something I know you've never done before..." I trailed off as his face flooded with colour, his gaze shifting to somewhere above my head. My eyes narrowed and I struggled to sit still. What was I missing here?

"Have you been here before? Does Pappy know?" My other father, Pappy, was the quiet type who only spoke if he felt the need, which wasn't often. Although when he did, everyone tended to listen. Even my father, who barely listened to anyone apart from Gwil's father.

It took a second to register the tension which rolled off my father as I tried to latch on to what I was missing. But for some reason, I couldn't quite grasp it. I sighed in frustration.

"Yes, to both questions. But this isn't about me or your Pappy." His sigh filled the silence, his teeth raking over his lower lip as he looked thoughtful. His eyes seemed to be calculating something. Before I could say anything though, he carried on talking, his voice dropping to a mere whisper. "The council have found out that I sent you here and they are not happy. They want you and Gwil brought back to Elvedom immediately."

His words shattered all hopes of finding out who I was. My stomach twisted into a hard, knotted ball, my heart thudding. "No. I... we... haven't done as you commanded yet," I stated, my mind frantically trying to come up with something, anything that would prevent our return home.

"Listen Son, I..." He hesitated, his hands raking through his silver mane and for the first time in living memory showing his agitation.

Shock reverberated through me as if I'd been struck by lightning. Dear Elvedom, what was this? Why was he so agitated? I scrambled out of the bed and ran over to my father, my chest tightening at the look of defeat in his eyes.

"You're frightening me, Father. What is this? What am I missing?"

CHAPTER TWENTY-ONE

Drake

What had gone wrong?

What had set Benidic off?

I shook my head. No matter how many times I went over it, I couldn't find the answer.

One minute he'd been voraciously watching me, and then the next—he'd gone nuts. I'd had no time to register what it was that had passed across his face before he'd shouted his safe word.

Fuck, he'd been so panicked that I'd been convinced he was going to rip off his balls. It had taken all of my strength to hold him still. And then he'd starting sobbing, tearing pieces out of my heart. Gwil's anguish had only compounded it further and I'd been torn over who I should comfort first.

I'd chosen Benidic, reassuring Gwil that I'd make it up to him once I'd figured out what had gone wrong. Only, even after removing the humbler from Benidic, he'd still been far too distressed to do more than shake with uncontrollable sobs.

The sight of his tear-stained face and swollen, miserable

eyes had been all it had taken to set Gwil off. I hadn't been much better as I'd carried Benidic upstairs, having to work hard to swallow past the ball lodged in my throat.

By that time, both men were snivelling messes. I'd encouraged Gwil to help me bathe Benidic, hoping that the simple task would help to settle us all. Benidic had calmed down at the feel of the hot, scented water and our gentle touches, but he'd remained steadfastly mute. He'd spent the majority of his time in the bath with his eyes closed, shutting us out. It was as if he couldn't bear to look at us and that had hurt far more than I'd wanted to admit. But I'd sucked it up, saying nothing as I'd dried him and tended to his bruised and painfully swollen scrotum.

When I'd finally tucked him into bed, he'd turned his back on us. That had been three hours ago and I was still nursing the same glass of scotch I'd poured before sitting down and intending to talk to Gwil. *How did that work out for you?*

I stared down at the top of his silver head as he lay sleeping peacefully, curled up in my lap. Gwil hadn't been able to answer any of my questions. He was just as clueless as I was about what had gone wrong. The constant ache in my chest was a reminder of how fucked up things had become.

Doubts crowded my mind, doubts about my own skills and my own ability to read a sub. How had I got it so wrong? A sigh escaped before I could stop it, my breath rustling Gwil's hair and making him stir, his hand tightening on the fabric of my T-shirt. I swallowed another sigh as he settled again, laying my head back on the cushion. I closed my eyes, hoping it would help to reduce the throbbing behind them.

The questions started again, my hand tightening around

the glass I was holding. What had set Benidic off? Had the pain been too much? I pushed that thought aside, recalling how aroused he'd been. No one could fake that. His cock had been rock-hard throughout, or at least until whatever had set him off had happened.

Had he been jealous?

My lips pursed.

Maybe?

It was the first time I'd really touched Gwil. Could that have been what had upset him? It didn't fit though, not with the panic I'd seen on his face. No, it wasn't jealousy.

Benidic loved Gwil. It was as plain as the nose on my face. I'd witnessed it time and time again. I'd witnessed the care and attention he lavished on him, the way he made sure that he had what he needed before seeing to himself. Even when Gwil had been moody with him, it hadn't stopped Benidic's need to care for him, the gentle touches still happening between them.

Snippets of their past conversations floated through my mind. Who used the term *Elvedom*? It was a weird arse turn of phrase that both men had used more than once. My lips thinned. Was it some sort of hip new term? I couldn't say I was up to date with the younger generation's vocabulary. Hell, it changed so often that some of the younger subs at the club sounded like they were talking double Dutch to me. Although, the fact I hadn't spent much time at the club recently could account for my lack of understanding of the terms used these days.

But what about *bonded*? The phrase got stuck on replay as I recalled how quickly Benidic had changed the subject after he'd used that word. What did bonded mean?

The throbbing behind my eyes that had started to

decrease, made its presence felt again as I tried to concentrate. It was a strange word to use. I mean who said "when we bond" rather than when we fuck, or even when we make love? But bonded? That wasn't something that just tripped off the tongue.

My eyes opened to slits, my body tensing as I stared down at Gwil. His expression was innocent, something I knew wasn't fake. Well, that was unless they were the best con men in the business. But, I didn't think so. My gut was rarely wrong. After all, it hadn't taken too much investigation to confirm my instincts about both men still being virgins. How was that even possible in this day and age? How many men were still virgins in their twenties?

How the fuck would you know? Normally the type of men you're interested in can't wait to get fucked.

A wry chuckle escaped, but then died quickly as it dawned on me how difficult that made everything. Needing to move, I placed my glass down on the small table on my left before carefully shifting with the intention of slid Gwil onto the sofa.

"No, Daddy," Gwil mumbled, his hands tightening further on my T-shirt.

"I need to pee, sweet baby. Just give me a minute. I promise I'll come back," I whispered into his ear.

There was a huffed sigh, but the hand holding onto my T-shirt did let go meaning that I could shift him onto the sofa. His head lolled back on the cushion as he curled up, tucking his hands into his chest.

I swallowed hard, quickly turning away to give myself a moment to gather myself. I walked into the hallway, pausing at the sound of heated voices coming from upstairs.

What the hell!

Even before my brain could catch up, I was running up the stairs. Who the fuck had got into my home without me knowing?

Breathless by the time I hit the top step, I darted towards the partially open bedroom door, ready for battle. Only, as I burst through the door, the air was vibrating with bold colours and... was that a man? But then all there was, was Benidic, standing naked at the end of the bed with a look of devastation on his face.

My hands shook as my mind worked to process what it thought it had seen. Had there been a man resembling Benidic, wearing a silk robe, stood right next to my bed? I wanted to laugh off the thought but, given the unfamiliar scent lingering in the air and the defeated posture of Benidic, I couldn't.

Exhaling a choppy breath, I placed my hands on my hips. "Care to tell me who the fuck you were talking to?" I growled, my eyes sweeping the room, but again finding nothing out of the ordinary.

Gwil's expression was miserable as he shook his head. "No one," he mumbled, his gaze lowering to the floor. My stomach nosedived at the obvious lie and I struggled to contain my disappointment. "Is that so?" I gritted out through clenched teeth. "Are you telling me that I was hearing things?"

His teeth raked across his bottom lip, his gaze remaining firmly rooted to the floor. "Well... it... you see—"

"Stop. I don't want to hear any more lies. Are you prepared to tell me the truth?"

He shrank into himself, saying nothing and looking conflicted.

The seconds bled into minutes during our standoff.

From the very beginning, there'd been something different about the two men. Yet, I'd ignored it because of my own needs. Was this all my fault for not trying harder to find out more about their background? But then, the few times I'd asked questions, they'd done a great job of evading them or distracting me. *You let your dick take charge, right along with your Dom side, is what you did.*

Enough was enough though; it was time for answers. *What if you don't like what you hear?*

Was that why I'd let them get away without talking? Was I that scared of losing... whatever it was that was growing between the three of us?

Nothing can grow between all of you unless you stop hiding, said that same unfamiliar voice, sounding frustrated.

Will you just butt out!

I would if you moved things along. You're running out of time, bond with them before...

Bond? What's that supposed to fucking mean for fuck's sake! Stop talking in riddles, man!

The voice, that wasn't mine, stayed silent, leaving my questions unanswered. A wealth of frustration left my body feeling as if it was strung tighter than a bow.

Was I having a breakdown? Was that it? Hearing voices, seeing things that weren't there? Was I in fact just dreaming all of this and I was going to wake up and find myself in an empty bed, in an empty house? The very idea chilled me to the bone, knots of tension taking over from where my stomach had once been.

I shut my eyes and took hold of my left wrist with my right hand, squeezing as hard as I could. The pain was bright and breath-taking, but I didn't let up until I was sure I'd left a bruise, panting as I slowly opened my eyes.

Benidic stood only a few feet away, his gaze on me and still naked. His eyes were huge, the silver standing out starkly against his pale complexion.

Okay, not dreaming. This is real.

Now what the fuck do I do?

My lips curled into a smile as I snuffled the cushion that smelt of Drake. The man smelt like heaven. Warmth tingled through me and I blinked my eyes open to search for the man in question. I vaguely recalled him mentioning that he was going to pee, but as I looked around I wasn't sure how long he'd been gone for, because I might have fallen back to sleep.

The dregs of sleep fled as I sat up, memories of what had happened in the playroom flooding my mind. Benidic... what had set him off? I rubbed my tired eyes as I attempted to gather my thoughts.

I'd been too distressed by him trying to stand with that contraption still attached to his balls to think about what had been wrong with him. Later, in the bath he'd shut both me and Drake out and, a deep-seated pain settling in my chest. The fact that his actions resembled what I'd been doing to him over the last few days only added to my woes. Was it payback?

Did it matter what it was? Benidic had obviously reacted to something, something that had made him act frantic. But what was it? I'd been too distracted by the feel of Drake's warm, wet mouth around my dick, Benidic had clearly been enjoying what had been happening if his dick was anything to go by. So what was it that had upset him?

My brows drew together as I stared into space, unable to find an answer. When the minutes lengthened and there was still no sign of Drake returning, I got up off the sofa and walked silently into the hallway where I stood listening. Met with nothing but silence, I headed up the stairs to check on Benidic.

I stopped short in the doorway. The two men were stood perfectly still, both wearing differing expressions, but neither of them could be described as happy, tension rolling off them in suffocating waves. Needing to ease it, I stepped between the two men, placing my hands on their chests. Benidic's heartbeat was so fast that it made my palm vibrate. His gaze moved to me briefly as I touched him, a flash of defeat in his eyes that made me exhale quickly.

Drake didn't look much better, his features set in grim determination. The caring expression he'd worn as he'd gently bathed Benidic was nowhere in sight. My hand trembled against the soft cotton of his T-shirt. "What happened?" I asked hesitantly, unsure whether I wanted an answer.

"Ask Benidic."

Drake's response was stilted. I glanced between them before focusing on Benidic. "What did you do?" I asked.

His silver brows rose, his brow furrowing with a mutinous glint in his eye. "I didn't do any—"

"You lied," Drake interrupted in a harsh tone. Benidic flushed all the way down to his roots, his gaze lowering and his lower lip trembling.

I cringed at the wave of anger coming from Drake, my

hand warming with magic, the urge to ease his discomfort an instinct. When Drake gasped, I reined it back in, silently cursing myself. "What did you lie about?" I asked in an attempt to distract Drake. But my heart flipped as Benidic's gaze returned to mine.

We'd never mastered being able to read each other's minds. We'd always felt like it was too intrusive so we'd avoided it at all costs. I regretted that decision though as Benidic's eyes attempted to express what had happened without words. I shook my head at the devastation on his face, blinking back the tears gathering in the corners of my eyes.

Dear Elvedom, what was I missing?

Drake took hold of my hand, squeezing it reassuringly before stepping back from us. "From day one, you've both avoided questions about yourselves. I've stupidly let it slide. I've let my dick dissuade me from getting those answers. Well, that is about to change. Both of you follow me." There was nothing in the way he spoke to indicate that it was a request that could be refused, so I took hold of Benidic's clammy hand and followed silently behind Drake as he exited the room.

I glanced at Benidic, silently asking what we should do. My skin itched and I wasn't sure I was going to like what was about to happen. He shrugged, his defeated posture doing nothing to ease the anxiety tripping me up.

My legs were unsteady as we walked down the stairs, along the hallway and into the playroom. The first night we'd been brought in here came to mind, only this time I didn't think I'd be getting to come. No, I had a feeling this was not going to be about pleasure. My hand tightened around Benidic's.

"Gwil, go and straddle my spanking bench and then lie

face down." Drake pointed to the bench in question as he spoke, his voice betraying nothing of what he was feeling.

Reluctantly, I did as he'd asked. At the feel of the cool leather against my heated flesh, goosebumps appeared on my skin. Turning to face both men, I flicked my hair back over my shoulder before resting my cheek on the leather headrest without having to be asked. I had a feeling that Drake was going to want me to see what was happening. That was confirmed as his eyes lit up with approval. But the warmth in my chest didn't get an opportunity to spread before his expression became shuttered and he looked away.

The corset I'd made mere days ago, a corset Drake had enthused over, was collected from the top of one of the huge chests. I held onto the memory of the praise he'd given us for it. I'd eagerly embraced every new responsibility he'd bestowed upon us. Seeing that with each new piece we'd created his despair had lessened and been replaced by hope, I'd wanted to help even more.

Now, as I watched him fondle the soft, magical leather, I wondered if all the hard work we'd done had been for nothing. The look of distrust that had been gone for days had reappeared once Drake had accused Benidic of lying. What had he lied about?

I willed Benidic to look at me, but he didn't, keeping his gaze on the wooden floor instead. I swallowed a sigh, nearly choking on it as Drake stepped close to Benidic and wrapped the corset around his body. Benidic's cock, which had been flaccid up to that point, started to plump and he groaned. It sounded tortured, but not in a bad way. More like he was being pleasured.

My hands buzzed with magic and I was sure that if I looked down, they would be shimmering with colour. Holy crap! What did that mean? Was the magic I'd imbued into the garment acting against Benidic's. Or was it something else?

My mind worked frantically to try and figure it out as Benidic's body flushed with heat, his cock fully erect by the time Drake had fastened him into the red leather corset. If he was aware of what was happening to Benidic, he showed no signs of it.

Drake moved Benidic's arms behind him and then weaved the leather straps at the top around his slender arms. His palms were held together in a prayer-like position in the middle of his back. Where they met, there was a brief glow, his whole body tensing and giving the impression that he was keeping his magic in check. Something that both of us seemed to struggle with, particularly in this room. Like it actively tried to tug it from our centre.

I shook off the idea when it made no sense. Drake pulled on the two remaining straps and led Benidic over to the couch. "Stand still," he said, before walking over to the bank of chests that I'd never had the courage to look inside.

I gulped as he opened several drawers, his face lighting up. He withdrew something from one of them. Oh, dear lord, what was that? As if ready to answer my question, Drake moved back over to Benidic. His gaze strayed to mine, the glint in his eye making them appear both dark and light at the same time. Taking a shallow breath, I waited for what was coming.

"If you two have been telling the truth... then Benidic will never have experienced what's about to happen." Drake raised his hand, eyeing the black, metal object he held before carrying on. "This is what's called an Assgasm, a chastity device." His fingers stroked over the part that I assumed housed a cock. Although, looking at Benidic's arousal I wasn't convinced it would fit. Sat at the base of the sleeve was a metal clasp that held a lock with a tiny key hanging from it. A petite object was curved behind it, about the length of a finger, but fatter and tapered at the end.

"It will give your prostate a nice little massage while it keeps control of your cock." The playfulness in Drake's voice made my dick jerk against the bench. He grabbed a bottle off the counter before returning to Benidic.

I shuddered, my arse clenching.

Drake dropped what he held on the seat, positioning Benidic on the couch facing me with his legs spread wide. I exhaled in a rush, my chest heaving and, for a moment, I was disappointed that he wasn't going to use it on me.

Don't be daft. You don't want to be made to wear that.

Don't I?

CHAPTER TWENTY-THREE

Drake

The weight of Gwil's stare helped to centre me as I picked up the two remaining straps of leather dangling from the corset Benidic wore. My hand trembled as I bent one of Benidic's pale slender legs and then the other, placing his feet on the edge of the sofa so that he had to lean back in order to keep his balance. His silver hair hung around his willowy frame, gleaming brightly against the red of the corset. His cock jutted forward, angry and aroused, enticing me to do more than look.

Moving my gaze to his legs, I gritted my teeth as I started to bind one leg.

You need to show them who's in charge.

Hadn't I done that already by taking their clothes away?

Like they didn't enjoy flaunting their bodies at you any chance they got.

After their initial request for clothes, they hadn't shown any anxiety at being left naked I realised, my brows rising. Had they been playing me all along? More to the point, did they have a friend helping them to make me think I'd lost it? But if that was the case, where the fuck had he disappeared to in the bedroom? No one vanishes into thin air. Maybe they were magicians?

I paused in the midst of binding Benidic's calf to his thigh. Was that it? Was this all an elaborate trick? Were they planning on having the last laugh at my expense?

My heart stilled at the thought they could have played me the same way Sonny had. A part of me refused to believe that that could be the case, shoving insistently at the part that doubted them. When I shifted my gaze to Gwil, all I could see though was... was what?

Devotion? Affection? Or was there more? His eyes glowed as if he could read my unspoken thoughts, my heart stuttering in my chest. I swallowed, working hard to keep my emotions masked, which was harder than expected when they were riding roughshod over me.

Ever since I'd found these two men in my home, I'd been unable to find my footing.

Stop lying to yourself. They were meant for you. You felt it the second you saw them. That sense of knowing that they belonged to you, that they fit who you are deep in your soul. But if you don't do something soon, you'll never know the bliss they can bring you. The voice filled my head and I froze at the desperation I could hear in it.

The sound of my knuckles cracking jerked me from my stupor, Gwil's face swimming back into focus. I let go of the end of the leather strap and stepped back, sucking in a deep breath, and then another when the first did little to loosen the tight band around my chest.

This was seriously fucking with my head.

That might be the case, but time is running out.

The bite of my nails in my palms and the ache in my

hands were constant as I tried to block out the voice that made my insides turn to jelly. Was time running out?

My gaze moved over the two stunning men, taking in their translucent skin, strange-coloured eyes, beautiful Elfin features and their long, silky hair that made them so striking and—otherworldly.

Stop overthinking it.

I closed my eyes, took two deep breaths to even out my breathing and then once I felt my heart rate settle, I opened them again. I stepped over to Benidic, who was slumped dejectedly against the couch. His cock was now flaccid and nestled between his open thighs. Had he felt my discomfort?

When no immediate answer came to mind, the chastity device caught my intention. I considered his unbound leg before reaching for the lube and the cock blocker. Not wanting to overthink it, I slicked up the black sheath, bending the soft silicone of the tapered butt plug to one side for the moment. If Benidic had never had anything in his arse, even a small plug would feel large unless I loosened him first.

I ignored the whimper that came from behind me as I slipped his limp dick into the sheath, Benidic freezing and his chest going still. His dick started to swell at my touch, so I quickly locked the metal ring around the base, chuckling as his face fell.

I put the key into the pocket of my shorts before focusing my attention on his unbound leg. The last thing I wanted was for him to kick out once I'd started to play with his arse. So without preamble, I bound his second leg.

After I'd finished, I stepped back to admire him and allowing Gwil to see. His sharp inhale further ignited my desire, my pulse thrumming with heady excitement. My skin tingled as my gaze roamed greedily over Benidic.

Leant as he was against the black leather couch, the deep red corset stood out. Wrapped around his slim torso, it cinched at the waist and displayed his pink, budded nipples as they peeked out at the top, enticing me to add some adornment. The leather bindings around his splayed legs showed off his pale skin to perfection. Fuck, he looked stunning bound for my pleasure.

Under my inspection Benidic's eyelashes fluttered open, his gaze remaining lowered. His posture had changed. The earlier dejection was gone, replaced by an eagerness to sit up and put himself on display, or at least as much as his bound body would allow.

My gaze shifted to his groin, the sticky residue left on my hand from slicking the sleeve of the chastity device reminding me that I was far from finished. I knelt down, making sure that Gwil had a perfect view of what was about to happen. With lube coating the slim plug and the fingers of my hand, I lifted the black silicone sheath containing Benidic's cock. "Ease down a little and move your bottom to the edge of the couch," I crooned seductively.

Benidic shuddered, goosebumps appearing on his exposed skin as he did as I'd asked. His chest strained as he tried to wriggle forward within the bindings. His arse hung off the cushion beneath him, his feet dangling in midair, the binds making it impossible for him to straighten his legs. His hair clung to his shoulders and he was flushed from head to toe.

"Do you need to use a safe word?" I gritted out.

"I'm blondie, Master, I swear," he whined, his gaze moving to mine for a brief second, his wanton need doing crazy things to my already overstimulated body.

I nodded, unable to speak past the ball of need urging me to pounce on him and fuck him into the couch. I lowered my gaze to his arse cheeks and using a lubed finger, traced a line down over his balls, feeling the silky texture of his skin. Sounds of choppy breathing filled the room and I wasn't sure which one of us it was coming from. I was transfixed by the pale pink pucker that twitched as my finger slid closer.

Benidic hissed as I caressed the wrinkled flesh, teasing the nerve endings with several gentle glides until his hole gleamed wetly with lube. His legs juddered and the hissing became louder.

I tapped him with my finger, increasing the pressure and eliciting several long, drawn-out moans from him. His hips rocked in an attempt to encourage me to do more. I bit my lower lip to prevent an evil smile from spreading across my face at what I knew was coming. I pressed harder, the muscle softening enough to allow me to slip the tip of my finger inside. When he bore down, my finger slipped in up to the first knuckle. At the tight cinch of his arse squeezing me, my cock bucked in approval.

Holy fuck!

"Oh Elvedommmmm! Ohhhh... it burnsssss soo gooodddd," he wailed.

It took all my effort to hold still as I checked in with him. "Are you still, blondie?" Sweat coated his face, his gun-metal grey eyes meeting mine. His mouth opened, but all that came out of it was a groan. His hips moved, my finger slipping a little deeper. Feeling his prostate under my finger, I gave a devilish grin as I grazed it again but more firmly this time.

His whole body shuddered, his legs straining in their bindings and his skin turning a rosy pink as he struggled.

"Do you like that?" I rasped, my arse clenching as my erection bucked hard against the fly of my shorts. The ache only added to my torment as Benidic's arse clasped me tighter as if he was trying to suck my finger even deeper into him. Giving him what he wanted, I eased in slowly, the tightness of his arse confirming his virgin status like nothing else could. The silky feel of his clenching channel worked to undermine my control as the knuckle of my finger bumped against his arse cheek.

Benidic quivered, grunted and moaned, his entire body juddering with need and I was in no better a state. The throbbing of my crotch became almost unbearable as Benidic rocked on my finger to give himself pleasure. Benidic's desire was doing a number on me, making me forget that this wasn't about giving in to his needs, but about discovering the answers I needed.

Deeming him ready for the plug, I removed my finger from his slick channel reluctantly. I moved the plug until it nestled against his wrinkled skin. He stilled instantly, his gaze moving down his body and his eyes becoming impossibly large as I carefully pushed the plug inside him.

A loud groan and the sound of skin sliding against leather behind me, drew my attention that way. About to glance over my shoulder, I stopped as Benidic whimpered, his head lolling back against the couch, his mouth hanging open. I jiggled the plug a little, making sure it made contact with his prostate and gaining myself another full body shudder and moan.

I lowered my hand, scrabbling to undo my zip so that I could slip my hand into my shorts. I took a tight grip of my turgid cock, the urge to come almost overwhelming. Struggling to think past the need, I increased my grip until my balls ached. Gasping for air, I shut out the sight in front of me. That did fuck all though, given the acoustics assaulting me from all sides.

My jaw ached as I worked at reining in my need. *Virgins, virgins, they're virgins!*

My brain latched onto the phrase on repeat. It did little to help though, not with the memory of how tight and silky Benidic's arse was competing with it.

Fucking hells bells!

Even though I couldn't pull a coherent thought together, my hips moved. The second Drake had slid his thick finger into my arse, I'd been lost in a world of pain and pleasure. The two merged together, the burn lighting up my arse faster than a flame to a candle. Breath-taking pleasure had spread through me and then when Drake had hit something in my arse, my whole body had thrummed with the magic of it. The first time I'd felt my magic moving inside of me, I'd felt invincible. But this, this was so much more. It consumed me, leaving no cell untouched by its bliss. *Was this what it was like to bond?*

Breathless, needy and out of control, my body had taken over, shutting out all rational thought. The burn was forgotten in the need to get more of the intense pleasure, making me want to beg that he should never stop. Then he'd changed his warm finger for the cold silicone and blown my ever-loving mind. The burn wasn't as bad after his finger, but it was still there as I'd panted and licked my dry lips.

I'd felt so full, but it still wasn't enough as Drake had moved the plug and rubbed it against that spot inside me.

All thoughts had fled while my arse danced its way to heaven. My cock had attempted to swell but the metal ring had held it captive, centring all the pleasure in my arse.

Assgasm? Was this what he'd meant?

I groaned and panted, a full body shudder moving the plug inside me. The slick silicone teased my channel and rubbed against its sensitive walls. My eyelids were hooded and my back stuck to the leather underneath me. My bound arms throbbed as I moved, digging into my back. I didn't care, I wanted… I wanted whatever it was that was building inside me like a dormant volcano getting ready to spew its hot lava everywhere. I wanted everything and I wanted it now.

My gaze moved to Drake. His grim expression, the hand down his shorts and his eyes screwed shut did nothing to help though. My heart soared at the fact that I'd made him struggle, that I was pushing him as hard as he was me. I shifted my gaze to Gwil as he groaned from behind Drake. He lay there panting, a layer of sweat sheening his skin. His pelvis thrust against the leather bench as he watched us with a heavy-lidded, desirous expression, his mouth hanging open.

I cried out as our gazes locked, feeling his hungry stare caressing my groin, my balls riding closer to my body and increasing my torment.

The noise must have alerted Drake to my problem because a second later, his stormy gaze landed on me before looking over at Gwil. "Tut, tut, tut. Did Daddy say you could do that?" His shorts shifted lower as he got up off the floor, revealing his erection. The purple, veiny head glistened, my mouth watering for a taste.

Gwil stilled as Drake faced him. The shorts slipped lower still as he strolled over to the bench, the firm muscled arse that was uncovered flexing. Once he'd come to a stop, Drake glanced down before shoving the shorts down his legs and kicking them off along with his shoes. Then he stripped off his T-shirt and threw that aside as well.

Oh, Gods yes!

The dark hair covering his solid muscles glinted in the light, his body flexing as he moved around the bench, eyeing Gwil like he was a veritable feast. He stroked down the length of Gwil's sweaty back, pushing his raven hair back over one shoulder. Gwil shuddered and my hips jerked at the sight of Drake's brown hand against Gwil's pale flesh. "Were you being a naughty boy?" Drake crooned.

The sound of his voice caressed me from head to toe, causing a ripple of pleasure in my arse which tortured my throbbing balls.

"I'm sorry, Daddy," Gwil answered breathlessly, his gaze firmly fixed on Drake.

"Are you?" Drake questioned, his hand moving down between Gwil's splayed thighs. Gwil groaned, his pelvis once again grinding down. "See, you're being naughty for Daddy. What am I going to do with you?"

The light in his eyes said he knew exactly what he was going to do, my pulse racing so fast that the air in my chest was held captive as I waited and watched.

"No Daddy, I'm a good boy, I am." Gwil sounded anything but as he moaned at the hand moving between his legs. I could only guess at what was being done to Gwil's cock.

"Really..." Drake trailed off as Gwil released another long, needy moan, his hips coming up almost in offering. Drake didn't need to be asked twice. His hand moved so fast that if I'd have blinked I'd have missed it, lifting before coming down hard on Gwil's backside.

"Ouchhhhhhhh... Daddyyyyyy," Gwil cried, his body jerking against the bench, but his arse lifting higher.

The sound of flesh hitting flesh filled the room, mixed with cries, moans and groans. At this point, I wasn't even sure who they belonged to as I panted and wriggled. The memory of my orgasm when I'd previously been bound poured through me, along with the need to come. Only with my cock confined as it was, the sensations were centred in my channel, each hip roll or jerk moving the plug in my arse and taking me ever closer. Yet, it wasn't nearly enough.

Tears slid down my cheeks as I was denied what I needed. All the while, Gwil cried out, his arse glowing red as Drake gave him exactly what I wanted.

"Please... please... Master, touch me too, please... I'll do anything, please," I begged unashamedly. Drake's hooded gaze met mine and my heart stilled for several seconds.

"Tell me who you were talking to?" he rasped out, his strokes to Gwil's arse fewer, but not stopping entirely.

My teeth raked across my lip before I chewed it. It was only when a metallic taste filled my mouth that I realised how hard I'd bitten.

"Tell me... *now*," Drake barked out.

"My father," I blurted out and both men froze. It would have looked funny with Gwil's arse up in the air and Drake's hand hovering above it, if it wasn't for the fact that both faces wore identical expressions of shock.

"What... the... fuck... game... is this?" Drake spluttered.

"No way!" Gwil screeched, lifting his head to search the room.

"It's not a game, I swear," I pleaded as Drake's face became unreadable and he lowered his hand onto Gwil's back, holding him still. "We are..."

Whatever I'd been about to say dried up on my tongue,

the same sensations filling my body as they had on the fateful day my father had sent us here.

"No... noooooooo!" The cry was too late though. The room disappeared, as did Drake. I closed my eyes in an attempt to pretend it wasn't happening, but familiar scents filled my nose seconds later.

"What's up with your face? You've been staring into that empty glass for the last hour," Richard said, bumping my shoulder from the stool next to me at the bar.

I glanced at his handsome face. His brow was furrowed and his usual warm smile was nowhere in sight. I didn't argue with him as I stared at the bruise on my wrist. It was the one I'd given myself two days earlier to prove I wasn't dreaming. Don't go there! *What, you mean to the place where two men disappear right in front of you? That place?*

My jaw clenched, the throbbing only increasing as my teeth ground together. Two whole fucking days, forty-eight fucking hours and nothing to stop the memory that I'd been holding Gwil's erection when he'd disappeared. He'd disappeared for fuck's sake! One second he'd been there, as real as me, and the next he was gone. Leaving only a lingering scent of sweat and warm leather behind where he'd been lying.

After frantically searching my home, all I'd found was the garments the two men had made, the clothes they'd been wearing on the night I met them and their scent on my bedsheets.

Had it all been an elaborate scam?

What, two men making *themselves disappear while you were touching one of them? How can that be a scam?*

I hadn't been able to switch the thoughts off, barely sleeping or eating as I worried myself sick with unanswered questions. It was only Richard ringing for an update on his order that had made me leave my home to come to the club tonight. Now I wasn't so sure it had been a good idea. With several drinks swimming around inside me, I was tempted to spill my guts to him. I eyed him speculatively. Would he think that I'd lost the plot?

"Okay, you're worrying me now. You're gonna break your teeth if you keep grinding them like that."

Richards's large hand touched my arm and I slouched before turning wearily towards him. "Something happened and... I have no fucking clue whether it was real or I'm having some sort of breakdown," I answered despondently.

Creases appeared around his eyes as he frowned, the pressure on my arm increasing. "Do you want to come to my office and talk about it in private?"

I was so lost in my misery that I'd paid no attention to the men having fun around me. I glanced around, blinking the club into focus. There were semi-naked men dressed in leather everywhere I looked. Some were participating in the pleasures on offer, others just watching. The scent of sex and leather which normally acted as an aphrodisiac did little to wake my libido. The joy I usually felt at spending time in this environment with likeminded people had disappeared.

I gave a disheartened sigh before looking back over at

Richard. Could I trust him? We'd been friends for years, but we'd never been that close.

"Listen, I've had an increase in members joining, due I'm sure to your bondage creations. So I feel as if I owe you. Come on, I swear I'm good at keeping secrets. I'm better than a priest," he quipped.

At his attempt to lighten the mood, my lips curved into a smile and I found myself nodding. "Okay." I held up my empty glass. "But we'll need more alcohol."

"Bill, pass me a bottle of whatever Drake's drinking and two glasses, will ya?" His brows rose as Bill handed him a bottle of eighteen year old Jameson's, but he didn't say anything as he stood.

I followed him, concentrating on keeping my balance as the alcohol I'd drunk seemed to have gone straight to my head. As I stepped into his office, I glanced around. Although the room wasn't overly big, the white walls made it appear larger than it was. The office housed a black work desk which contained a keyboard and two large computer screens. There was a black leather seat behind the desk that looked well-used. Two more practical looking chairs sat in front of the desk.

The organisation in the office with nothing out of its place reminded me of my storeroom.

Stop right there.

My feet sank into the plush grey carpet as I walked over to one of the empty chairs and plonked myself down. Slumping, I rubbed my face before looking over at Richard sat on the opposite side of the desk. His expression didn't change as he poured two drinks, pushing a glass towards me.

I picked up the glass and took a sip, taking a moment to

gather my thoughts while I savoured the smooth taste of the alcohol. "I don't know where to start," I muttered.

"Is this connected to Sonny?" he asked hesitantly.

"Nah, why?" My brows rose when Richard's expression darkened.

"I... well, I never trusted him." He shrugged nonchalantly, but his face hardened. "He was only ever after your money. I never got why you couldn't see past the false facade."

"Me neither. But I've had a lot of time to consider it over the last couple of days and I think I was lonely. It had been a couple of years since I'd had a sub or a boy before him and well, he seemed to be what I'd been searching for," I said, shrugging. "Only it was all fake. But by the time I realised that, he'd already sucked me in." My mouth dried at the thought of how well he'd fooled me. I took another sip of my drink, hoping to remove the bitter taste from my mouth.

I brooded silently for a minute before pushing it aside. I couldn't change the past. I stared at Richard over the rim of my glass. "Do you believe there is... more to life than we know?" I blurted out, not sure why I'd felt compelled to ask that.

Richard's brows rode up his forehead as his eyes widened, the air in the room seeming to thicken. I drew in a shaky breath. He placed his glass down, propping his elbows on the desk in front of him, his gaze thoughtful as he licked his lips. "Yes, yes I do."

I resisted the urge to squirm beneath his penetrating stare. Instead, I clutched the glass, holding my breath as I sensed he was far from finished.

"Do you know how long I've had this club?"

Uncertain where he was going with this, I shook my head.

"Twenty four years. I inherited it from an uncle. My father was dead-set against me following my uncle into the BDSM lifestyle." He gave a self-deprecating laugh. "I'd been a member of the club for two years by then and it would have taken more than a stick of dynamite to get me out." His gaze moved around the room as if he was seeing it for the first time. "This place called to something inside me. It took me a while to figure out that it held... magic." The last word was said with such reverence that it seemed to hang in the air between us.

I shifted in my seat, my heartrate tripling as I squeezed the glass, needing to feel its weight in my hand. "What... what do you mean... magic?"

His searching gaze met mine, my stomach twisting into a tangled mess. "I think you know what I mean. That leather bondage gear that you brought me... What do you feel when you touch it?"

The alcohol that had been buzzing through me seemed to disperse as quickly as an effervescent tablet in water, sobering me instantly. The glass rolled against my sweaty palm. The seconds stretched as I struggled to answer truthfully.

"You can trust me, Drake. I swear on Elvedom, you can."

The glass slipped from my lax fingers, and although some part of me acknowledged that I'd just spilt alcohol all over my leather trousers, I was too stuck on Richard's choice of words. *Elvedom!*

Had Richard somehow set me up?

I shot out of the chair, the glass rolling across the floor to land against one of the legs of the desk, a dark stain appearing on the carpet.

Leaning over the desk, I got into Richard's face. "What

the fuck kind of game is this? Did you set me up? Did you send Gwil and Benidic to me? How the fuck did you make them disappear—"

He shoved me backwards towards the chair I'd vacated, stopping my rant. He held his hands up to ward me off as I regained my footing and went to attack him, his biceps bulging. "Stop this fucking nonsense! I have no idea who Gwil or Benidic are," he ground out. "Sit your fucking arse back in the chair and let me answer what questions I can. But you need to listen to what I have to say before you ask me anything else."

There was something about his tone that turned the knots in my stomach to lead, but I found myself doing as he'd requested. Once I was seated again, I had to bite my lower lip to stop myself from demanding that he talk.

"You asked me before whether I believed that there was more than we can see and I answered truthfully, I do. But there was a time I'd have scoffed at you... but that was before... before I got a visitor from another realm —Elvedom."

The sincerity in his face matched his voice, and as much as I wanted to shout at him to stop the bullshit, a part of me accepted what he was saying as the truth. Hadn't I always thought that both men appeared otherworldly? But coming from another realm? How was that possible?

"When I first started to visit the club, my uncle talked about a magic portal to another realm. I laughed it off, thinking he'd had one too many spliffs and was talking crap. But then one night, I was in the dungeon enjoying the show when a... man sat next to me. Fuck, he was my biggest wet dream all wrapped in leather trousers. His skin was translucent and his long flowing silver hair was like a silk cape draped over his chest. I was instantly mesmerised."

Richard's expression turned distant as he continued to speak as if he was completely unaware that he'd just ripped the rug out from under me. "He didn't talk. He just sat there, watching me and the men on stage. He left after an hour, but returned several nights later. He never spoke to me though, and somehow it kept me from saying anything. For weeks he'd seek me out and sit quietly next to me, tempting me with his scent and his willowy body. Then one night he came while I was flogging a sub. He stared at me as if I'd betrayed him in some way."

Richard shook his head, his lips curling up at the corners. "He made me pay spectacularly for that betrayal. Anyway, what followed was a discovery of what it's truly like to connect with a sub. To understand how making my sub fly gave me flight too."

He sighed, running his hands through his thick, mahogany hair, the flecks of silver catching in the overhead light. He focused on me. "He still makes me fly with him, all these years later."

The meaning behind his words had me out of the chair and pacing over to the door and back. Was he talking about Benidic? The description matched, but Benidic could only be in his twenties.

I scratched my bristly jaw. "How many years have you been seeing this... man?" I paused for a second to look at Richard.

"Twenty three years," he answered without preamble.

"Then why have I never seen you with him?" I thought about all the times I'd visited the club, realising that I'd never seen Richard play with anyone—ever. I started to pace again. Why had I never noticed that Richard was always alone?

"Tristan doesn't age the same as us, so it made it more

difficult to conceal our differences as the years passed. So we've kept our relationship behind closed doors for the last decade, to prevent any questions about him and what he is."

Richard paused to lick his lips, but I'd hardly registered anything else that he'd said after the name Tristan. I collapsed into the chair as I reached it. The relief at the fact that Richard hadn't been talking about Benidic after all was immense.

Richard shifted to the edge of his seat, taking hold of my icy hands. "Tell me about your... men. And I'll explain what I know."

My pulse thundered in my ears as I started to talk about everything that had happened, while secretly praying that Richard would be able to give me the missing answers I needed.

After a furtive glance down the opulent hallway of the palace, I ran towards Benidic's bed chamber. My silk robe billowed around me, the soft fabric rubbing sensuously against my skin. I bit my lip to stop a moan from escaping as I opened the door without knocking and darted inside.

My chest tightened in despair at the sight of Benidic lying on rumpled silk sheets, his hair a mess and his face all red and blotchy. His eyes stayed closed, but his body twisted away from me. Hurt stabbed at my heart, my feet dragging as I walked towards the ornate bed.

The past few days had been hellish. Any thought that living on the streets of London had been the worst thing that could have happened, had been erased by this new misery.

When I'd finally come to my senses and realised that I was being pulled back to Elvedom, I wasn't sure whether to be more mortified about being naked, or about being aroused. It had been a close call. However, the council of select Elves who assisted in ruling the realm had seemed more bothered by the sight of Benidic in his bondage outfit.

Therefore, I'd been spared too much scrutiny, the council's outrage directed solely at Benidic. Him dressed in leather, wearing a cock cage and with a plug up his arse was way more than they'd been able to handle.

Yeah, it hadn't been a fun time, that was for sure. Top of the list of things to do had been untying Benidic in front of watchful eyes, only to remember that we didn't have the key to the chastity device he wore. Thankfully, tapping into my magic had worked and I'd made the cage and plug disappear before too many questions could be asked, or before the council had got close enough to inspect Benidic.

Although, the expression on a couple of the council member's faces had said that they would have loved to get closer to a naked Benidic trussed up in leather. Later in my chamber, I'd questioned those stares, wondering how much information in the kingdom was kept from young elves.

Rubin, a weasel of an Elf with mean eyes had started to spout off about the king not being fit to rule. He had issues with him having sent us to the earth realm, and with him having a son who was... how had he put it? Depraved, that was it. At that point, I'd been forced to seek answers.

That had been three days ago, but with Benidic taking to his bed chamber and refusing to eat, drink, or *wash*, it had been hard to stay focused on finding out what was going on.

My nose wrinkled as I got to the edge of the bed and the smell of sweat met my nose. "Get up and bathe, you stink. I've got some news to share, but I'm not going to do it when you smell worse than three-day-old garbage."

"Get lost!" Benidic said in a flat tone.

I yanked at the silk covering his body and, before he

could evade me, tugged on his bare arm to drag him from the bed.

"Stop that. I said get lost," he wailed, his legs kicking in my direction.

I avoided being kicked as I continued to pull him from the bed. My heart skipped several beats as he stared at me with red-rimmed eyes and my heart ached for him. "You need to stop being a selfish bastard. You're not the only one suffering here. I lost Drake too," I demanded, keeping a firm grip on his arm, needing him to understand that this wasn't just about him.

He stood, sagging against me as he pulled at his arm until I let go. He wrapped himself around me, burying his face in my neck and exhaling shakily. "I'm sorry," he mumbled into my hair.

I sighed, holding him close. "I know you are. But this wallowing has to stop. I might have found a way to go back—"

I didn't get a chance to finish as Benidic pulled back and started to throw questions at me. For the first time in days, his ghostly pale face became flushed with colour. "What? How? Oh Elvedom! Are you serious?"

"Jeez, how am I supposed to answer if you won't shut up?" I complained, but he still didn't listen. He ran towards the bathroom and I shook my head before following him.

I stopped in the doorway, taking in his thinner frame. How much weight had he lost? My gaze travelled to his face as he looked my way. There was a gauntness to his features that I hadn't noticed before, but under the gleaming lights I couldn't miss it.

Emotions that were impossible to control rose up, and I took hold of Benidic to give him a little shake. "This punishment you're inflicting on yourself, it stops now. Do you hear me?" I gave him a harder shake before pulling him into me. "I need you to be healthy. And so will Drake when we go back to him," I said, my conviction born from the visit to the same Elf Benidic had got the taboo book from.

I nudged him towards the bath. "Wash and I'll explain what I've found out."

The smile he offered was the first real one I'd seen in days. Feeling a little lighter, I perched on the padded chair in front of the vanity chest where Benidic loved to preen. I chewed my lower lip between my teeth as I waited for him to get into the scented water, using the time to organise my thoughts into some semblance of order.

After what had happened in the main hall and the Elves' whispers about things I didn't understand, I'd gone in search of answers. My love of history had led me to the archives where the old records were stored, records that I'd never been encouraged to read and it hadn't taken me long to figure out why.

There in the pages had been a reference to portals that Elves had been using for centuries to travel back and forth between the two realms. This destroyed my misconception that only those on the council, or the king, had the magic required to go between realms.

There was even mention of Elves mating and bonding with human males and that this had brought about an uprising, resulting in a divide amongst the Elves. Some believed that the lineage of Elvedom should remain pure, whereas others believed that Elves needed to travel to the human realm to find their human mate to complete their triad.

This had struck a chord with me, the part of me that had always struggled with not being enough for Benidic rejoicing at finding a possible answer. I thought about Elves in a triad. But, it didn't take long to realise that triads had become a thing of the past.

Was that since they'd locked down the portals? Could they not find their thirds now that they couldn't visit the human realm?

The sound of splashing pulled me from my thoughts and I focused my gaze on Benidic, who was eyeing me with more than a little concern. "I've said your name no less than four times and you've not answered me once. What's wrong?"

"I'm sorry. I was trying to put my thoughts into order so that I can explain what I discovered from the records and from talking to Cassius."

At the mention of Cassius, Benidic picked up the cloth from the side of the bath, along with the bar of scented soap, feigning interest in what he held. His hair fell around his face as he lathered up the cloth.

"There's no point in hiding from me. I know what you did. In fact, I know *everything*." I knelt at the side of the bath, letting the excitement I'd been working so hard to contain in front of others, bubble up. My hands fluttered at my sides so I held on to the side of the bath as I explained what I'd found out.

CHAPTER TWENTY-SEVEN

Drake

When I got to the door of my workroom, I stopped, shutting my eyes before reaching for the door handle. Had they been? *Open the bloody door and find out, you idiot.* My hand shook, slipping on the metal knob as I sucked in a tremulous breath and entered the room.

I walked over to the bench on unsteady legs, my gaze fixed on the shoes in place of the leather I'd cut out the night before. I stared at the dozen pairs of handmade shoes on the bench. Each pair was more exquisite than the previous, the stitching impossibly neat, making it difficult to tell whether they had been handmade or not. But I knew.

My vision blurred as I reached for the pair closest to me. Blinking rapidly, I swallowed as the familiar tingling sensations spread from my fingers and through my arms as I examined the miracle I held.

The shoe design was just as I'd imagined. The pair of pink ladies' court shoes I held had delicate flowers in several shades of green interwoven into the leather.

I sniffed as I caressed the soft leather, hoping to get rid of the burning sensation in my sinuses. Using the back of one hand, I swiped at my eyes. My gaze swept the room to see whether anything else had been touched. But it looked just the same as I'd left it with nothing out of the ordinary. Well, unless you counted what was on the bench in front of me.

Fuck. Fuck. Why didn't they show themselves to me? Six days! Six whole bloody days and I still hadn't seen either man... or Elf. *They aren't men; they're Elves!*

My fingers tightened on the leather as I recalled everything Richard had told me.

"*I know this sounds far-fetched Drake, but these men are Elves. They live in Elvedom and can travel between their realm and ours. They've been doing it for more years than either of us could count.*"

I went back to pacing, my mind screaming at me that I must be in a remake of 'The Twilight Zone,' only they were adding 'Lord of the Rings' as well just to spice things up. All I needed now was Legolas to come through the door dressed in bondage gear and ask me to be his Dom!

Richard sighed. "You know deep down that I'm telling the truth, don't you? You felt a connection to Gwil and Benidic beyond anything you've ever felt for anyone else. I'm right, aren't I?" He got up, stopping me from pacing by holding onto my arms. "These Elves are your soulmates, your bonded ones. I know it's a lot to take in. I've been in your place. It's a hard pill to swallow, to find out that there is so much more than we know, but Tristan and Luka brought me some of their history books." He gave a wry chuckle. "They were a real eye opener."

His hands tightened on my arms. When I looked into his

eyes all I could see was honesty staring back at me. The weight of it pressed against my straining muscles as I let everything he was saying sink past the fear that I was going mad.

Was it that conversation that had started the visits in the middle of the night?

God only knew! And did it matter in the grand scheme of things?

I shook my head.

After his confession, I'd left Richard and gone home to try and figure out what it all meant, and what, if anything, I was going to do about it. With thoughts of Richard running through my head, I'd gone back to my first love: shoes.

Since the disappearance of the Elves, I hadn't been able to work on anything connected to BDSM, so it had been a relief when the shoe designs had come easily. I'd spent an age figuring out which shoe designs I wanted to cut out first. But after cutting the leather pieces, I'd been too tired to start hand stitching them. So I'd left the leather sitting there, only to find a pair of shoes where the leather had been in the morning. They'd been a perfect rendering of my vision. Recognizing Gwil and Benidic's craftsmanship immediately, I'd been elated. With my heart racing, I'd called out, searching the entire building in the hopes of finding both men, only to come up empty-handed, my elation turning to devastation.

I'd sat for hours afterwards staring at the pair of shoes, unsure what they were trying to tell me. When I'd cut more leather, the pattern had continued. Each morning I'd wake to find shoes made from the leather I'd cut. On the second and third night, I'd tried to stay awake, but when I woke it was to find myself slumped in the chair with a crick in my neck and no sign of them. The only indication they'd been were the shoes sat where the leather had been.

Even though my front window now resembled the shoe shop it had once been, I struggled to embrace the happiness without...

A sob choked me and I dropped the shoes back on the counter so that I could cover my wet face with my hands. Why were they not showing themselves to me? The question continued to hammer at my brain. Think goddamnit!

I scrubbed at my face, something niggling at the back of my mind. What was it Richard had said about a magic portal?

Was there really a magic portal in Richard's club that allowed Elves to travel from their realm to ours? And if so, would I be able to use it to go there and get my men... my Elves back?

Exiting the taxi, I groaned at the long queue of men standing on the pavement. I racked my brain trying to remember if there was an event tonight. Those usually drew a big crowd. Richard planned a monthly event to showcase one of the kinks, some of which I'd participated in over the years. Passing the crowd, I walked up to the door, nodding at the doorman.

Wick stood around six feet four and was built like a tank. He was an intimidating presence. "Hey Wick, how's it going?"

"It's all good, man. Ya after jumping the queue?" His blond brows rose, his blue eyes sparkling with humour as they moved from me to the long line of folks behind me.

"Yeah, I need to see Richard about... something important." Hoping he'd not caught my hesitancy, I let out a relieved breath as he opened the door.

"Go on in, but ya owe me one," he rasped out, a devilish smirk on his face that I wasn't sure I wanted to question. I'd never quite figured out what Wick was into. He tended to hang about in the background just watching, making me wonder if he was into voyeurism.

I stepped into the foyer to be met with a wall of heat. Within seconds, sweat was sliding uncomfortably down my back. Shrugging out of my coat to reveal my leather harness, I stood in line to pay to have it stored in the cloakroom.

Afterwards, I eyed the two doors in front of me, opting to go into the dungeon rather than the main club room, Richard's story about the night he'd met Tristan in the forefront of my mind.

The sound of metal whizzing through the air and the scent of cum assaulted my senses before I managed to get my bearings in the dimly lit room. My gaze swept the large crowd flocking around the stage as my eyes adjusted. They were watching a Dom use a metal beaded riding crop on his sub. All eyes appeared riveted on the sub, who was mewling and writhing against the spanking bench with every delicious stroke that hit his naked buttocks. His cock and balls had been pulled down between his splayed thighs with heavy weights, giving the Dom the perfect target to strike.

My body reacted to the visual, blood surging into my dick as I imagined how Benidic might look in the same position.

"I wasn't sure I'd see you again," Richard said quietly, touching my arm to draw my attention to him. His expression was guarded as he held out his hand. "We all good?"

I took his hand, squeezing it while I nodded. "Yeah, we're cool. But," I glanced around to see if anyone was paying attention before continuing, "I have some questions about the... you know what."

His brow furrowed for a second before smoothing out. He chuckled, tugging on the hand he still held to draw me to the back of the room out of ear shot. "You want to know if you can go into their realm, right?"

CHAPTER TWENTY-EIGHT

Benidic

My breath hissed out between my clenched teeth as I glanced over at Gwil, wanting to curse him for the umpteenth time.

"Go slow," he'd said, "Let's give Drake some clues as to what we are," *he'd said!* Well I was fed up with what *he kept saying*. I wanted more than words. I wanted action. Because where had the last week got us? Bloody nowhere, that's where!

Only tonight, after the longest week in history and finally managing to get Gwil to agree to reveal ourselves, Drake was nowhere in sight. The moment we'd snuck in through his back door, I'd instantly sensed the building was empty. The leather was there on the work top, all neatly cut out waiting for us to make the shoes, just as it had been ever since the first night we'd followed the instructions Cassius had given us to get back to London.

The dark alley we'd found ourselves in had initially given little away. Then we'd found ourselves outside a club. Closer scrutiny of the men queuing outside had revealed no less than two pieces of the bondage wear I'd made for

Drake. Only that wasn't the only thing I'd discovered, *hell no*. There in the crowd had been one of the top Elf council members clinging to a big leather-clad Dom. It was laughable that Elves were using the portal to get their baser needs met while acting all high and mighty at council meetings.

I'd fumed silently, Gwil yanking me out of sight and back into the alley and reminding me why we were there. After using magic to create the pounds we'd need to pay, we'd hailed a taxi.

"Where do you think he's gone?"

I shrugged, wrinkling my nose at Gwil. "How would I know? I've suggested every day that we wake him up to talk, but no, *you* said to wait. Well look what happens when we waited!" I grumbled loudly, not caring how petulant I sounded. Something struck me, my heart trembling. "What if he's gone to find some other men to be his boy and his sub?"

Gwil's face fell, tears shimmering in his eyes as he stared at me. "Do... do you think he'd do that?" His voice trembled, as did his chin.

"I don't know. He gave up trying to catch us after just two nights." I stared at the leather on the bench. "Maybe he's only interested in the things that we've been making for him." The leather corset I'd donned before dressing in the jeans and jacket rubbed against my sticky flesh as I turned my back on the counter.

"Stop it, he's not like that—"

"Oh really, you've got a short memory. Were we not held here against our will naked, while he got us to make leather bondage goods for his clients?" My hands moved to my hips as I tapped my foot on the wooden floor.

Gwil rolled his eyes at me. "Give over. It wasn't against our will." His face turned a deep shade of red. He coughed as I arched a brow. "Okay, don't look at me like that. I'm talking about the fact that we stayed. We chose to do that regardless of what your father did." He pointed at me accusingly. "And I'd just like to point out that you loved roaming around naked so that Drake could look at you. You were so hard, your dick could have hammered nails into wood. I never heard you complain once, apart from on that first day."

"Alright, there's no need to go on. We need to figure out what to do now, not rehash what I did or didn't do." I sighed despondently. "We only have a few hours before someone will check on us. What are we going to do now?"

Gwil's gaze swept the room, his eyes narrowing.

After the humiliation I'd endured in front of all the senior Elves and my father, nerves danced over my skin at the thought of getting caught breaking the rules. My father had barely said two words to me since. The air of disappointment he wore when he looked at me had left me feeling confused and heartbroken.

When he'd shown up in Drake's bedroom, I'd sensed that he'd been about to explain why he'd sent both Gwil and me to the human realm. Only Drake had put the kibosh on it. Now that my father had to prove to Rubin and the other council members why he was a fit ruler for the realm, he had no time for me.

Given the information Gwil had uncovered though, I wondered if his responsibilities were an excuse to avoid me. My suspicions had only grown at the knowledge that Father and Pappy were spending a lot of time apart. I'd begun to notice a lot of things about them that I hadn't before. A lot of things didn't add up. Like how they both appeared to be subservient towards each other. Their behaviour was reminiscent of my own with Gwil. There was genuine affection and love between them, but there seemed to be something missing? Were they supposed to be a part of a triad?

From the brief time we'd spent with Drake, my guess would be yes. Drake's presence had added an element that we'd needed to close the divide between us, to form a three-dimensional bond that made us whole.

After Gwil's revelations, I'd finally been honest about what I wanted and what I felt was missing from our relationship: Drake. Gwil had been just as open, and after a few tears we'd started to think about how we could get what we wanted.

The only problem was, we weren't sure how my father sending us to the human realm fitted into it. I couldn't explain it to Gwil, but I felt like it was important. I just hadn't figured out how, yet. All we knew for sure was that there was a Drake-sized hole in our lives and it seemed the fates, or my father, had tried to ensure it was filled.

A shiver raced down my spine as I imagined never being able to get back what I'd had with Drake and Gwil before it had been snatched away from us by Rubin and the council.

I shook off the concern, refusing to believe that once we found Drake, we wouldn't be able to be with him, now and forever. My breath caught in my lungs as Gwil swung around, his hair shifting around his slender frame, the light making it look like polished onyx. His face had never been more beautiful than it was with determination shining from his eyes.

"I love you," I murmured, stilling as his head turned in my direction and his gaze met mine.

There was such a wealth of emotion swimming in his eyes that I felt like I was drowning in them.

"I love you too, Benidic, with all that I am." His confident tone did silly things to my heart as he offered me a sassy grin. He started to open the drawers of Drake's desk where I'd seen him store his paperwork.

My brow furrowed. "What are you doing?"

"I'm looking to see if there is anything in here that will give us a clue where Drake might have gone." He stopped rifling through the drawer to glance up. "Make yourself useful and create the shoes for Daddy. We don't want to start off on the wrong foot, do we?"

I didn't see any point in responding, not when Gwil had already switched his attention to the open drawers. I rolled my eyes heavenward at the bossy side Gwil had started to demonstrate and tutted. Glancing down at my twitching dick, I groaned. It seemed to appreciate the bossy behaviour a little bit too much. *Give over. You love being told what to do.*

Unable to argue, I stepped up to the bench. My fingers traced over the soft, scented leather as I lifted them. I moved from piece to piece, pictures forming in my mind. Once I'd handled them all, I closed my eyes, letting the images form before allowing my magic to surface. Tendrils of magic tugged at my core until they gently subsided and I opened my eyes. A smile spread across my lips when I saw the shoes lined up in front of me.

"I've found something, and you'll never believe it!"

I turned around in response to Gwil's excitement. "What is it?"

His brows rose. "The bondage wear we've been making is for that BDSM club where the portal brought us through. I don't think that's a coincidence, do you?"

The nerves returned, my hands trembling. "No, I don't. Do you think that's where Drake has gone tonight?"

"We won't find out unless we go and check it out. And

at this stage I don't think we've got anything to lose." Gwil shut the drawer before walking back over to me and taking my hand.

At the warmth and weight of his palm against mine, I nodded. "Let's go."

We'd taken no more than three steps towards the doorway when Gwil froze at my side, his chest barely moving. I glanced between him and the door to the hallway, straining to listen. Had Drake come back? Or had the Elves realised we'd left the realm? My heart stuttered in my chest, my fingers tightening around Gwil's as a scraping metal sound was followed by a brief rattle and the *swish* of a door opening.

CHAPTER TWENTY-NINE

Drake

I threw my keys on the table in the hall, barely resisting the urge to kick at its wooden legs as I passed. The black mood which had slipped into place from the moment that Richard had informed me that the portal could only be opened by magic wouldn't leave me. It hung around like a bad smell, contaminating everything in its wake. The subs at the club had scattered like ants when my gaze had landed on them. Any thoughts of staying to enjoy the second show had died when a sub had walked onto the stage wearing one of the bondage outfits Gwil had made.

Cursing myself to hell and back, I'd stomped out of the club and hailed a taxi. But now I was home I had no fucking idea what to do next. I'd clung to the hope that Richard would be able to help me, praying that if I could go... wherever my men, *my Elves* were, that I'd be able to find them and persuade them to come back with me.

At the end of the hallway, I glanced into my workroom and skidded abruptly to a halt. My tongue glued itself to the roof of my mouth, my heart jackrabbiting against my ribs. "Fucking bullocking shit!"

Oh fuck! Oh fuck! Please let this be real. Please!

With my gaze firmly fixed on the two men whose eyes were the size of the saucers, I was barely aware of moving towards them. The thundering pulse hammering in my ears said I wasn't imagining them. But as I got to within inches of them, I stopped. I blinked twice, lifting trembling hands to reach out and cup their cheeks. My sigh was tremulous, the feel of their warm, smooth skin beneath my rough palm making it painful to swallow.

"You're real."

"Yes," they replied in unison, alerting me to the fact I'd spoken aloud.

Gwil's eyes sheened with tears while Benidic's were full of concern. I removed my hand from Benidic's cheek to take hold of the back of his neck, clasping it tightly. Silky strands of silver hair rubbed against my flesh and made it tingle.

He sucked his lower lip between his teeth, gnawing on it.

"Stop biting. You'll bloody your lip by gnawing on it like that," I growled, still unable to believe that they were here in front of me. The time it took for him to do as I asked and lower his gaze, was only seconds but felt longer than an hour. My heart soared as he melted into my hold showing me what he wanted.

I glanced at Gwil, but his gaze was fixed on Benidic, the tears gone and in their place a feverish light I recognised.

Nerves I wasn't used to feeling sprang to life and I strained to keep control. The raging need to claim these men and take what my heart deemed was mine reared up like a cobra ready to strike. My tongue felt thick, making me swallow hard as I dropped my hands back to my sides.

Registering their confused expressions, I balled my hands into fists in an effort to prevent myself from reaching out to soothe them. "Why have you come back?" I demanded in a husky voice.

"Daddy, we didn't want to go, I swear. You have to believe us, they... the... well, you see..." Gwil trailed off, licking his lips as he looked at Benidic from the corner of his eye. But Benidic remained looking down, his face having lost its colour at my question. Gwil huffed and met my gaze. "We're Elves!"

"Way to go Gwil, just blurt it out," Benidic whined, glowering at Gwil.

"What was I supposed to say? Tell me? And I'd just like to point out that you weren't helping!" he said, his hand lifting to swipe at the tears sliding down his cheeks.

Their little disagreement broke the tension in the room like nothing else could have, their bratty behaviour a soothing balm to my battered soul. I fastened my twitching lips into a straight line before taking the step that separated us. I tugged Gwil into my side while taking hold of Benidic's nape again. "I know what you are, well sort of. But whatever you are, it makes no difference to me. What am I going to do with the pair of you?"

"Whatever you like, Daddy," Gwil answered breathlessly.

"What he said," Benidic added, peeking at me from beneath his eyelashes. His body was quivering with pure need, his cock pressing firmly against the fly of his pants. Gwil was in the same position.

"Are you sure? Because once we start down this path there's no going back. You'll be mine *forever*." I emphasised the forever, hoping they'd get that I understood why they were virgins without me having to go into the conversation

I'd had with Richard. He'd told me how Elves bonded through anal sex, that once they were joined in that way there was no way to break the bond.

I'd lain awake night after night imagining what it would be like to have a lifelong commitment with not one, but two... *Elves*, and although I was apprehensive about it, a part of me desired it.

The tension in my shoulders released as I received two vigorous nods. Benidic reached out and took hold of Gwil's hand connecting the three of us. Spirals of colour glowed around them, spreading over my body and leaving tendrils of pleasure in its wake.

"Wow!" I exclaimed, my dick throbbing with the urge to come in my leather pants without so much as a single touch. I wheezed, scrunching my eyes shut as I attempted to regain the control that their combined magic was stealing from me.

There were sounds of giggles as I took deep breaths to gain some semblance of control. My hold on myself still tenuous, I opened my eyes. "Are you two being naughty?" I growled, but without any heat as two pairs of eyes stared at me full of... love.

Was I imagining it? Or was it real?

A ball of emotion lodged itself in my throat and I licked my lips.

It's real! Humans, why do you need to question every-thing? Get a move on before someone discovers that they have gone.

The sense of urgency in the voice sent a shiver of apprehension down my spine. Instead dof questioning it, I accepted what it was telling me. Sending up a silent prayer that I wasn't going to live to regret what I was about to do, I released my hold on both men. "Strip."

They didn't hesitate. The next thing I knew there was a

pile of clothing on the floor of the workroom. My eyes widened at the deep blue corset Benidic wore, saliva pooling in my mouth. "Did you get dressed for me, sub?" I crooned in delight, tracing a finger across the soft scented leather which covered him from just above his hip bones to his chest. The leather cinched in at the waist making it appear tiny.

Intricate patterns that matched his hair were weaved in silver thread across the main body of the corset. The leather had been cut so that it left his nipples exposed, my imagination running wild with the thought of how the pink buds might look pierced.

Benidic shuddered, his chest heaving as he gave a slight nod. The silver mane of his hair shifted around his shoulders, brushing against the back of my hand. I glanced round the room. Spotting a small piece of leather strapping lying on my workbench, I went over and retrieved it.

I offered the leather to Gwil. "Plait *my sub's* hair."

The leather was snatched out of my fingers eagerly, forcing me to swallow a chuckle. Gwil's hands glowed purple as they threaded through Benidic's silky strands, weaving them into a complicated braid. I stood transfixed by the pattern he was creating. Was it magic or just creativity? Did it matter? It was a part of who they were.

Once he'd tied the leather at the base of plait hanging down Benidic's back, Gwil gave me a happy grin. "Is that okay, Daddy?"

"It's beautiful. Thank you, sweet baby." I shifted so that I was close enough to brush a soft kiss against his mouth. His lips parted in an invitation which I was only too happy to accept. His familiar sweetness invaded my taste buds as I deepened the kiss. I couldn't stop myself from pulling him against me. His tongue tentatively stroked against mine in an erotic dance of innocence that stole my breath away.

Breathless and achingly hard, I lifted my head. At the sight of his dazed violet eyes, my heart swelled. Warmth spread through me, banishing the coldness that had lived inside me ever since both men had disappeared from my life. As if sensing my emotions, Benidic pressed himself to my back, his hands settling on Gwil's waist. It only registered that I still wore my coat when Benidic rested his forehead on my back.

"Benidic, be a good little sub and take my coat off." He let go of Gwil, taking hold of the zip of my jacket and fumbling as he attempted to blindly tug the zip down.

Gwil's mouth opened at the sight of the leather harness I wore, but no sound came out. I glanced down at my chest and chuckled. This was the first time either man had seen me dressed in my Dom gear. I stood a little taller as Benidic peeled my jacket off. Gwil's gaze roamed over the harness before lowering to my black leather trousers which fitted like a glove.

"You like Daddy dressed in leather, don't you, sweet baby?"

"Oh Daddy." He squirmed, his hand lowering to hover over his erection.

"You know the rule, sweet baby. You don't touch unless Daddy says so."

His lower lip poked out, his hands dropping reluctantly to his sides. I struggled not to laugh at his petulant expression.

CHAPTER THIRTY

Gwil

The need to argue died at the spark of mischief in Drake's eyes. The gloomy expression he'd worn before registering our presence in his home was long gone. I'd all but swooned at his feet as hope, and something more profound had appeared on his face. But all I could think about now was what was going to happen next.

Benidic and I had talked about what we thought might transpire. Well, we'd hypothesised. Neither of us were exactly sure what Drake would do with the hard cock behind the leather of his trousers. The website had given us an idea though. My arse clenched and my dick bucked. Drake's eyes shifted to my groin as my hands moved restlessly at my sides.

"Is my sweet baby getting impatient? Now that will never do." His gaze moved to Benidic, who seemed just as anxious as me, his body quivering.

The gorgeous blue corset shimmered in the lights and I longed to touch. I spoke without thinking. "Daddy can I touch your sub, please." I wheedled, fluttering my eyelashes.

I didn't miss Benidic's sharp inhale, but I continued to stare at Drake, pleading silently.

"I think it's time we took this to the bedroom so that we can make use of the big, comfy bed I have." He didn't wait for an answer before swinging around and walking over to the door with us following quickly behind. He didn't look back, heading straight into the room and turning on the lamps at the side of the bed.

I halted with Benidic at my side, eyeing the bed cast in a soft glow. The part of me that wanted what was about to happen became lost beneath the fear of the unknown. What if Drake didn't get what this meant? What if I'd got it wrong and he wasn't our third?

He is. You know he is. It's just nerves, that's all.

Drake beckoned us towards him, the panic in my head deciding I was in some sort of race, one where my thoughts chased each other. The feel of Benidic's fingers clasping mine was followed by the caress of his magic against my skin. Pleasure spiralled through my body, ungluing my feet from the floor as Benidic tugged me over to the end of the bed with him.

Once there, Drake began to unbutton his leather pants. He paused, a smile that should have been outlawed spreading across his face. "Undress me."

Benidic didn't need to be asked twice, dropping my hand so fast that it was as if I'd burned him. He skipped over to the bed and was on his knees before I could blink.

Not wanting to be left out, I stepped over to Drake before hesitating. "Can I take off your harness, Daddy?"

His eyes became hooded, but he nodded. The only sign of how much this was affecting him were the choppy breaths which brushed my naked skin. Careful to avoid trapping the hair on his chest, I undid the buckles that held the harness around his shoulders, dropping it on the floor beside Benidic.

He didn't acknowledge the soft *thud* as it landed beside him, too busy taking Drake's boots off. I took advantage of the opportunity to run my hands over the springy, dark hair smattered with silver that covered Drake's broad chest. A shudder wracked Drake's large frame as he exhaled, his pecs moving under my gentle touch. His dark brown nipples pebbled, my mouth yearning for a taste.

I glanced at Drake, trying to gauge whether I'd be allowed to do as I wanted. Passion and need swirled in the depths of his eyes and I swallowed. Taking hold of my courage before it deserted me, I sucked the budded nipple between my lips. A groan rumbled through my chest as I savoured the flavour of his skin in my mouth. He thrust his chest forward, pushing the nipple deeper, my cheeks hollowing as I sucked harder.

"Fuck!" he groaned, sounding as if he was in agony. "Yeah, fuck. Do it again."

So I did. Only this time, I took hold of the other budded nipple as well, going with instinct as I pinched it hard between my fingers as I bit down on the nub in my mouth. There were more curses, Drake's large hands cupping my head to hold me in place. Warmth filled my chest at being able to give this man, *my man*, pleasure.

I was so heady with the power surging through me that it roused my magic and it began to flow without restraint. My body hummed with it, intertwining with my love as they melded together. These two men made me whole in ways I'd never imagined possible. The painful wait to be reunited with Drake, to claim what Benidic had understood before me, melted away as I explored Drake's solid chest.

My hands and mouth traced each dip, each ridge of muscle, secretly marvelling that I was free to do so.

Benidic's hand stroked down my flank and I moaned as his magic merged with mine. They danced together playfully, heightening my arousal.

Breathless, I pulled my head back, crying out as wet heat engulfed my dick. My hips jerked as I looked down at Benidic's pewter eyes. The desire and love etched in his face was more than I could take as his tongue licked over the head of my cock, seconds before swallowing my cock down his throat. He choked, his eyes streaming, but refused to give up his prize.

A shudder rippled through me, my hips jerking forward to seek more of the delicious pleasure riding through me. I moaned as cum jettisoned out of my dick. My mouth hung open, my entire body quivering as I was held in the grip of mind-bending desire.

Benidic sucked harder as if he wanted to suck me dry, his lips opening and pulling back as the last spurts of cum hit his face. Drake yanked Benidic up, pulling me against the side of his body as he took Benidic's mouth in a hungry kiss. His grunts and growls as he tasted my cum caused shivers to spread across my body, my dick thickening again as it got ideas. It was as if it knew that this was only the beginning.

Euphoric sensations thrummed through me as I avidly watched Drake lick the cum off Benidic's cheeks and chin before he turned to me. "Kiss me, taste yourself."

The very idea aroused me to the point of pain. I stood on my tiptoes, doing as he'd asked. My tongue swept into his mouth and I moaned at the slightly bitter essence mixed with the taste of Drake and Benidic.

Oh my! I ground my lower body mindlessly against Drake's hip needing something to ease the throbbing.

"Such a needy, sweet baby. But Daddy doesn't remember saying you could come," he whispered against my wet lips. A ripple of delight ran through me at the glint in his eyes magnifying my need.

"Daddy... I'm sorry, but it was Benidic's fault. He was the one who sucked my dick." I gave him a shamefaced smile while happily throwing Benidic under the bus, knowing that whatever punishment he got for sucking me off, he'd love it.

Drake chuckled as he looked at Benidic. Benidic gave a mournful sigh and hung his head, but not before I'd seen the excitement he couldn't hide.

"Then I'll need to do something about that, won't I? But first, sweet baby, I think you should take off Benidic's corset."

CHAPTER THIRTY-ONE

Drake

Benidic's cock dripped with excitement as he stood naked in a pose of submission, waiting to see what I'd do after Gwil had shoved the blame his way. I'd felt that heavenly mouth on my dick so I couldn't really blame Gwil for losing control. Add in the crazy, magical buzz that the two Elves had going on and I was surprised I hadn't come too. The added facet stroked over my body like little pulses of electricity lighting me up like the damn Christmas lights at Covent Garden.

When Benidic started to fidget, I shifted my gaze to Gwil, a vivid image of him fucking Benidic while I fucked him filling my mind. I couldn't get past it as it became fixed in my head. Walking over to the bedside cabinet on unsteady legs, I opened the drawer to retrieve the lube.

Richard had assured me that I didn't need condoms. My jaw clenched at the thought of sliding into Gwil's virgin arse while he did the same to Benidic. The bucking cock pulsing between my legs was also totally onboard with the idea. I swallowed a sigh, praying to God that I wouldn't embarrass myself by coming the second that I was inside him.

Lube now in my hand, I hoped like fuck I'd be able to prepare both men without losing control. "Both of you bend over the end of bed side by side." I inhaled, holding my breath as I waited to see what they'd do. When neither hesitated, I let go of the breath I held, taking the few steps needed to climb on the bed so that I was in the middle of both men.

At the sight of their translucent skin glowing in the lamplight, I placed the bottle of lube down before gently stroking the pert globes of flesh. Small whimpers and groans followed my touch, their backsides lifting.

By the time I was done touching, my cock had slicked my thighs. I gritted my teeth against the need to plunder and take. This was more than just fucking and I wanted to make their first time an experience that neither would forget. Determined not to let my dick lead, I tamped down on my own desire as I lifted the bottle of lube. After parting first Gwil's and then Benidic's thighs, I swallowed hard at the sight of the pale pink holes that were mine to do as I wished with. I tipped the bottle, pouring a liberal amount of lube down both of their creases.

"Ohhhhh," Gwil cried.

"Shitttt," Benidic groaned, burying his face in the cover.

A chuckle became stuck in my throat as I dropped the bottle on the bed, running the tips of my finger over their puckered flesh. They moaned, encouraging me to continue to tease them. My fingertips slid in the wet liquid, spreading it around their entrances before pushing gently on the rings of tight muscle simultaneously. The long drawn-out groans that followed could have come from either of them as I concentrated on giving both men pleasure.

behind Benidic. His thighs pressed against Benidic's, his red cock pressing against one of his pale arse cheeks.

There was a flash of uncertainty in Gwil's eyes as he looked at me. "Daddy... you want me to... fuck, Benidic?" His voice trembled, but his eyes held mine for a moment before moving away nervously, only to return a second later.

"Don't you want to sink your cock into Benidic's tight arse? To feel all those muscles clenching around you like a silk glove, and feel how much he wants you?"

"Oh," Benidic's eyelids fluttered, along with the hands he held at his sides as he took hold of Benidic's hips.

CHAPTER THIRTY-TWO

Benidic

The heat rolling off Gwil penetrated my already overheated body. His cock felt like it was branding my arse as it lay heavily against my sensitive skin. Once Drake had asked Gwil if he wanted to stick his dick inside me, I was ready to beg for mercy. My hole quivered at the idea of being filled with more than Drake's digits.

By the time he'd finished fucking me with his fingers, every part of me felt like it was throbbing with need. I ground my hips back against Gwil, not caring if I appeared desperate. Because quite frankly if someone didn't stick their dick in me soon, I might have to take matters into my own hands and impale myself on one of them. Either man would do; I didn't care which one.

As if Drake could read my mind, his mouth brushed against my ear. "Take a deep breath and bear down."

A shiver rippled down my spine as I did as he'd asked. The cock that had been branding my arse slipped between my arse cheeks, nudging at my hole. Tiny flickers of pleasure flooded my ass as there was pressure against the rim. I gasped, my eyes stinging from the sweat that slid down my face as I embraced the burning feeling like a long-lost lover. With every inch that sank into my body, the burn spread until that was all that was left to take my mind off the fullness in my arse.

Wave after wave of immeasurable pleasure thrummed through my channel, making me feel more alive than I'd ever felt in my long life. My heart soared and any disappointment that it wasn't Drake who'd claimed me first fled as Gwil's hands tightened on my hips, his groin touching my arse.

What in Elvedom, is this? My arms shook with the need to clutch my chest as it filled with fire. A raging inferno derailed everything else as it built to a crescendo stealing my breath away. My teeth ground together as I tried to fight past the sensations that felt bigger than me and the two other men in the room combined.

Panic flared deep inside me, at odds with the need. *You want this, you do, embrace it.*

Holding on to the thought, I bit my tongue to stop a safe word from flying out of my mouth, tasting blood. Was this what the Elves had warned me about? Pain and fire, was that what they'd said? It had to be. I tried to remember but as the next wave of fire moved from my chest to my limbs, it took all of my effort to be able to think past the raging blaze holding my body in its thrall.

As if I was an observer, I felt Gwil's pelvis push against my arse, his hot breath ghosting over my back. But then my magic started to hum and vibrate through me merging with the fiery heat.

Drake's hands stroked across my arse cheeks, his slick thumb circling the stretched skin of my arse before pushing in beside Gwil's cock.

"Argghhhhhh... Whatttttt... Fuckkkkkkk!" I wailed at the top of my lungs. My chest heaved as bright, bold pain replaced the burn. Throwing my head back, I carried on howling, driven by insanity to move as my body sought out more of the punishment. I needed it more than I needed my next breath, the pain and pleasure mixing as I writhed in an ecstatic state of bliss.

"That's it, search for the pleasure." Drake crooned in that husky voice that made me want to beg. His thumb slid a little deeper as Gwil's hips thrust, the tiny movements driving me mad.

"More, harder, oh Gods I'm on fire," I cried, the tears leaking down my heated skin giving me a second of cool relief before dripping on the bed.

"We're going to give you everything you need." Drake's voice sounded further away, prompting me to glance back over my shoulder. My arms nearly gave way at the expression on Gwil's face as Drake knelt behind him and ground his body against Gwil's. Drake's thumb stayed buried in my arse, his other hand reaching around Gwil to take hold of his hip. The disappointment at not being able to see what Drake was doing to Gwil fled as the pressure in my arse increased and it felt as if Drake was actually pushing his cock inside me as well as Gwil's.

"Holy mother!" I yelled.

Gwil moaned loudly, thrusting deeper into my arse, Drake's thumb stretching my arsehole even wider. Eyes watering, I struggled to suck in a breath past the pain, past the pleasure. I shook my head in an attempt to clear it, my arms giving way so that I fell forward. There was no time to brace myself, my face becoming buried in the covers. The hands on my hips tightened as I moved my head to the side, sucking in greedy breaths.

But it wasn't nearly enough as Drake thrust deep into Gwil, who in turn thrust into me. Lights flashed in front of my eyes. Noises disappeared, apart from the buzz in my ears as the fire returned to my chest searing even hotter and making me believe I'd been tossed into hell. It consumed me whole stealing my ability to breathe.

My body shook, intense pleasure starting to override the fire with each powerful stroke of Gwil's and Drake's cock. It radiated from my arse, spreading into my balls and down my cock. Then it was game over as Drake's thumb slid free from my arse. Gwil shifted over me, pressing his sweat-slicked chest to my back, his hands pressing against my heart. His magic merged with mine in hot pulsing waves, crashing through me and tearing my body apart only to put it back together. In its wake was an indelible imprint of Gwil and Drake where once there had only been me.

As if that wasn't enough to be dealing with, Drake's deep voice commanded, "come," and as if my body had been waiting just for that instruction, my dick jerked hard, hot bursts of cum soaking the cover. I quivered as each pulse fired from my cock, my heart rejoicing at the exquisite pleasure running rife within me. Gwil's body juddered against mine, heat searing my arse as he gave a strangled cry in my ear.

The pleasure intensified leaving me mindless and incoherent as I finally felt Drake come. He might not have been physically inside me, but that didn't seem to matter as my channel convulsed and I was sure that I could feel his seed pulsing inside me along with Gwil's. Shivers ran over my skin, my cock doing its best to continue to spurt cum in an effort to show its appreciation.

Holy Elvedom, if this was the mating bond I wanted to do it again and again. Heck, I never wanted to stop doing it.

Exhausted, I sank down onto the mattress, my legs shaking. Drake leaned over both of us, blanketing Gwil and me with his heavy body and pressing us deeper into the bed. I released a contented sigh even as I struggled to take a breath. My eyes drifted shut and I soaked up the feeling of contentment knowing I'd found my place. I'd found what had been missing from my life—a Drake and Gwil sandwich.

As my mind came back online, I registered an odd, achy burn still lingering in my chest. I huffed when the sensation wouldn't abate and I found it impossible to settle. "You're squishing me," I gasped breathlessly, both men thankfully rolling to the side. It was only then that I caught sight of Gwil's chest. My eyes widened, my heart fluttering as I rolled onto my back and sucked in a breath before glancing down.

What... what the heck happened?

I scrambled to sit up, my fingers hovering over my chest where the intricate bright blue triangle marked my skin. If that wasn't enough to contend with, the air shifted. I groaned as the room filled with the council of Elves and my father.

Oh Elvedom!

CHAPTER THIRTY-THREE

Drake

Initially, I was too distracted by Benidic's alarmed expression and the fiery sensation in my chest to register that there were several Elves standing at the bottom of my bed.

The scent of herbs filled the room, along with the sound of swishing silk. The long robes they wore were as bright as a rainbow, long hair of varying colours flowing over their slim shoulders. Their appearances were too similar to Gwil's and Benidic's to fool myself into believing they were anything other than Elves.

It was only when I noticed the interested stares aimed at Gwil and Benidic that I realised we were naked. My heart thundering, I snatched at the cover yanking it from under both men and tossing it over their naked bodies.

"What the fuck are you doing in my home?" I ground out, my hands warming and lights flickering from my palms.

Holy fuck!

That caught everyone's attention, but I was too busy freaking out at the tattoo that had appeared right over my heart. The dark blue and purple colours stood out prominently on my chest. *Motherfucker!*

My fingers trembled as I went to touch the mark, the purple and bluish light sparking from my fingers eliciting several gasps and chuckles. I glanced towards the group at the foot of the bed seeking out the fucker who thought this was funny, only to be met by a face almost identical to Benidic's. *Oh, this just gets better and better.*

As if the Elf sensed my rising anger, he took a step closer. "I'm so sorry for the intrusion on this momentous occasion. But as this is a bit of delicate situation I'm hoping you'll forgive us..."

I hadn't heard one word he'd said after sorry as I recognised the all too familiar voice which had invaded my head, the one that had been encouraging me to take things further with my Elves.

"Why?" I demanded, stopping him mid spiel.

His face alone showed understanding and I struggled to swallow as I tried to decipher what it all meant.

"This situation is preposterous. You've allowed this to happen right under the noses of the council. Look, look! They all bear the triad symbol. How on Elvedom are we going to undo this?" screeched a weaselly looking Elf, all but foaming at the mouth as he sneered at the Elf who had to be some relation to Benidic.

Heat pulsed from the mark as my hand covered it, both Gwil and Benidic groaning in unison. As my gaze moved between the two men, I noted that they bore the same mark, only Benidic's was blue whereas Gwil's was deep purple. The intricate symbols the triangle held made no sense to me, but it seemed to mean something to the screechy man, that was for sure.

"Stop speaking rubbish, Rubin. Magic this pure can

never be broken. A triad bond is the most sacred mate bond, as you are well aware. And if you took your head out of your ancient arse and stopped trying to keep things as they were, you'd be able to see the beauty in this mating."

"My head out of my... what!" The urge to cover my ears competed with the inane urge to laugh at the squealing, red-faced Elf.

"Tristan, you have become complacent in ruling our kingdom. See what it has led to." Rubin glared at the two Elves sitting frozen next to me. An ugly sneer marred his mouth as he continued to rant. "Your son is depraved and you have done nothing to—"

The room vibrated as if we were about to experience an earthquake.

"I'd advise you to think carefully about what comes out of your mouth next. There is nothing depraved about the needs of the soul. I'm sure the other council members will attest to that too." Tristan's stare was hard as he met each Elf's gaze.

By the time he returned his gaze to Rubin, there was a lot of squirming going on. Rubin's face lost its colour as four of the Elves nodded in agreement.

"What is this?" Rubin spluttered.

"You've been using the uprising and your petty jealousy to cajole others into seeing things your way and it stops now. Times are changing, Rubin, and if you're unable to move with them, then I shall remove you from the council." The finality of Tristan's words garnered several nods. Rubin looked around the group of Elves as if he was seeking support, but all he got was a wall of disinterest.

"This is all great. And I'm glad that you guys are sorting your shit out. But can you get the fuck out of my home now, so that I can have a little chat with Tristan?" I stated, working on keeping my tone civil.

Something niggled at the back of my mind as I said his name, but it disappeared as Benidic shifted beside me.

"You need to be careful how you speak to the council of Elves," Benidic mumbled, glancing from me to his father. His shoulders slumped, his hands clutching at the cover.

"They might be a council of whatever, but this is my home and the only person in charge here is me, got it?" I took hold of his dipped chin and stared into his eyes. All the happiness that had been there earlier was gone, and my heart ached with the need to replace the misery. "Who is in charge?" I asked.

Benidic's nostrils flared as he shifted on the bed, his eyes darting first to his father and then back to me. He sucked in a breath and whispered only loud enough for me to hear, "You are, Master."

Emotions blinded me for a second as he offered up his mouth, his whole attention focused on me.

"That's right, I am, and later on I'll make sure to remind you of that."

He shuddered, his gaze becoming heavy-lidded as his tongue swept over his lips. He gave a slight nod and I lowered my lips to his claiming his wet mouth in a brief kiss, conscious of the Elves still watching us. Gwil groaned and I released Benidic's swollen lips to give Gwil a devilish smirk. "What, sweet baby?"

He scooted closer to Benidic, his eyes begging as he offered up his mouth. "Me too, Daddy."

There were gasps and sharp inhales, but I ignored them in favour of giving my brave boy what he wanted. After I'd released Gwil's sweet mouth, I shifted my gaze to Tristan. "Are you all after a peep show? If you continue to hang around, you'll end up getting the show of your lives." My brows arched as Tristan squirmed uncomfortably, while the others' expressions showed a lot more eagerness with the exception of Rubin, who continued to glower at anyone who looked at him.

"You can leave, I'll stay and talk about what happens next." Tristan made a shooing motion with his hands and as quickly as the group had arrived they disappeared.

I settled back against the headboard, tugging Benidic over my legs and nestling him into my side while pulling Gwil into the other side of me. Once I had both men tucked happily against me, I gave Tristan my full attention.

I gestured to the chair in the corner of the room. "Sit, and then you can explain what the hell has just happened."

Tristan lifted the chair and placed it next to the bed before getting comfortable. His robes shifted, the scent of herbs wafting in the air. "I'll start with an apology. I'm sorry for my devious actions, but I was left with no other option."

His silver brows pinched together as Benidic flattened himself against me, his fingers clutching at my chest where the tattoo was and making it throb.

"Benidic, you are so much like me, and I didn't want you to suffer the same as Pappy and I did until..." He trailed off, his gaze becoming distant as he continued to speak. "Having different needs is not wrong or depraved, and I've hidden for far too long due to small-minded Elves who think the uprising fixed something that wasn't broken. What they couldn't see was that the uprising stopped Elves from seeking their human triad mate and that Elvedom's magic has ceased to flourish the way it used to with our human bonded mates. When I saw Drake, I sensed immediately that he belonged to you and Gwil, and I—"

"Excuse me, you saw me? When? How?" I lurched

forward, both men clinging to me. The niggle was back, only this time stronger than before. My eyes narrowed on Tristan.

"At the club you frequent... I was there when you came in one night." He shrugged his slim shoulders, but his pinched mouth showed that he wasn't as unaffected as he was trying to lead me to believe.

The moment he mentioned the club something clicked in my head and my eyes widened. "Richard is—"

"Is none of your business," he growled, his face becoming an unreadable mask.

When Benidic stiffened, I let it go, the need to take care of him overriding everything else. He whined in distress and buried his hot face in my chest. "Shush baby, it's alright, I've got you." I glared at Tristan. "Spit out whatever it is you want to say. Then go so I can comfort *my* Elves."

His eyes lit up with humour and, if I was right, respect. He lounged back on the chair as he continued to explain how he'd gone about giving Benidic and Gwil the opportunity to have what the council would have denied them if they'd figured out they had a human mate.

By the time he'd finished, Benidic was weeping, Gwil stoically offering silent comfort as he stroked his hand.

"Is that *everything*?" I questioned. My brow rose as he nodded. But then his head tilted towards Benidic and he shook his head. The meaning was clear. Benidic couldn't take any more revelations. Not right now.

Grudgingly, I gave a small stilted nod. "If that is everything, I'll ask you to leave."

He got up, hesitating at the side of the bed. "I'm truly sorry, Son, for not sitting down and talking to you about all of this."

Benidic shifted, leaving a damp patch on my skin as his

teary eyes met his father's. "I'm sorry too for causing you so many problems."

"Yes, you really are a hellion, but that doesn't make me love you any less." Tristan's eyes sparkled with love. "I regret that I didn't have the courage to share the side of me that would have allowed you to flourish..." His gaze moved to Gwil. "...to make you understand that there wasn't anything wrong with your bond with Gwil. It was just that it needed something else that Elvedom couldn't offer." His face grew sombre. "A triad mating will change your DNA, Drake. The symbol on your chest is only the beginning."

He chuckled as he rubbed his chin, the sombreness departing as he stared at me. "Elves live long lives and yours will now match both Gwil and Benidic's. I hope you know what you've let yourself in for. These two can be a real handful."

"Oh, don't worry. I'm sure I'm more than capable of keeping them both in check."

Tristan roared with laughter, his face alight with humour. "I'm sure you're man enough. I'll leave you now. Please bring Drake to the palace once you've talked every-thing over." He waved, disappearing as quickly as he'd arrived.

I glanced at both Elves. There was a moment of hushed silence before Gwil and Benidic both started talking at the same time.

"Did you have any clue what your father was doing?"

"How is it possible he knew I was part of a triad just by seeing Drake?"

"Stop the pair of you. Does it matter how you came into my life?"

Both of them shook their heads, offering up sheepish grins.

"No, Daddy," answered Gwil.

"No, Master, answered Benidic, a cheeky grin forming on his face.

I shook my head. "All that matters is that we have each other, the rest we can work out as we go." As I spoke, they joined their hands over the triad symbol tattooed on my chest. The air pulsed with colour, the hand holding theirs warming and pulsing strangely.

Holy fuck! That really was going to take a little getting used to.

"We're your Elves and you're our bondage Daddy, isn't that right?" Gwil asked earnestly, his eyes glowing with more than magic as he stared at both of us.

"It is right." Holding them closer, I kissed the top of each Elf's head as I whispered, "Now and always, my loves. Now and always."

EPILOGUE

Drake

SIX MONTHS LATER

The bell over the door rang and I glanced up from the counter where I was serving a customer. A smile spread across my face as my father walked through the door. His gaze moved around the shop, a look of approval on his face before it landed on me.

He nodded, waiting for me to finish with the man who'd come to buy his wife a pair of shoes she'd seen in the window and had raved about for days.

It had been like this for months, ever since I'd made the decision to reopen the shop. With the window full of unusual shoe designs, it had drawn a daily crowd of shoppers more than willing to part with their pounds for something just a little bit special. The one-off, bespoke shoes were such a hit that my Elves had to work hard to keep the shelves stocked.

Not that they minded when they were rewarded daily for their efforts. I chuckled at the memory of how competitive they'd become, wanting to out-magic the other with a design that not only earned my praise, but the customer's as well.

Once the man had bustled out of the door with a smile on his face, clutching his bag, I arched a brow at my father. "What brings you in today? I thought you and Mum were coming on Saturday for dinner?" I tidied the ribbon away that I'd used to tie around the shoe box.

"These shoes remind me of your great-grandfather. He loved handcrafting fancy designs on leather," he said wistfully, picking up a shoe that had caught his eye from one of the shelves as he passed. His fingers rubbed over the leather —once, and then again.

My heart sped up as I watched him. His pewter grey hair was swept back off his forehead and his weather-beaten face wore a thoughtful expression.

"You know they feel the same too," he said absently, shaking his head.

"What do you mean they feel the same?" I asked, holding my breath.

My parents had accepted Gwil and Benidic, not that my father hadn't expressed some concern about me being able to keep one person happy, never mind two. I'd brushed over it giving a vague answer that I had nothing to worry about. I mean, how did someone explain to their parents that they were the bonded mate of two Elves that were more than a hundred years my senior?

Yeah, that was something I didn't even want to contemplate. *Hell*, some days I found it hard to understand it myself. Especially when the magic buzzed to life and I was given a stark reminder of just how lucky I was.

"The leather feels alive, like it's full of magic." He

laughed, his cheeks filling with colour. "I said that once to him too and he laughed at me, but I got this odd feeling that he knew exactly what I meant."

As my father looked from the shoe and then back to me, I shrugged as nonchalantly as I could manage with my guts twisting into balls of anxiety at the thought of lying. So instead I went with at least part of the truth. "They are magic. My boys helped make them, so as far as I'm concerned they're full of it."

He placed the shoe back down and shook his head "Don't say shit like that in front of your mum or I'll never hear the end of it. You know she's always going on about how crap I am at that romantic nonsense." He was grumbling, but his face lit up as he spoke about my mum.

"You're just jealous that I've got a silver tongue—"

"I can confirm that," Gwil said, grinning as he came through the back of the shop carrying several boxes. His face radiated happiness.

My heart fluttered in my chest and I hoped I didn't have the same sappy expression on my face as he did.

"Jeez, look at you," my father moaned, killing my hopes.

"Shut up, old man, and tell me why you've come into town on a weekday when you hate it?"

"Hey less of the old. And I'm here because I'm fed up listening to your mum going on about a son that has a shop full of bloody fancy shoes and she has none."

His mournful expression made my lips twitch. Gwil giggled as he dropped the boxes on the counter.

"I think I might have something that will stop her complaining," Gwil muttered as he rifled through the boxes he'd brought into the shop. The furrows on his forehead disappeared as he pulled out a beautiful pair of ankle boots.

If I was right, they'd be a perfect fit for my mum and were in her favourite turquoise colour too. Delicate hand-sewn flowers were woven into the outside of the boot which resembled flowers in her garden.

My father took the boots from Gwil to examine them. I rolled my eyes at Gwil, but he gave me a sly wink. I was convinced that the bugger had just used his magic to create them in order to please my father. But all I could do was smile at his impish expression as he stared at my father with a hopeful look on his face.

Two seconds later, Benidic appeared, his face flushed and a guilty look on his face. In his hands he held a suede handbag that matched the shoes. I shook my head at the way they were tag teaming my father, keeping my amusement from showing. Benidic was standing a little awkwardly, as he often did when he wore a cock cage for being disobedient. He'd test the patience of a saint with his antics, his own father often laughing about how it was my problem to deal with now.

Given that I got the benefits to dishing out punishments, it was hard to see a downside to Benidic testing the boundaries to see what I could dream up next for him. Gwil's need to please balanced us out, making things all the more exciting as he eagerly watched me work Benidic over until he cried for mercy. Then Gwil would join in and torment him too. They were the perfect balance of dark and light.

Fuck, I was one lucky bastard.

Before Gwil and Benidic, if someone would have asked if I could have my cake and eat it too, I would have probably said no. Yet, here I was, with two Elves that couldn't do enough for me, a thriving business and to all intents and purposes a very long life to enjoy it.

Benidic's excited voice interrupted my thoughts.

"This bag is a perfect match to the boots. Maybe Maria would like this too?" He gave my father a winning smile as he all but snatched it out of Benidic's hand like he might take back the offer.

Handbags were something that my boys had decided we needed to branch out into and I'd said *very clearly* that I'd think about it. I eyed the bag, Benidic's gaze refusing to meet mine.

"This will keep me in her good graces for months." Father eyed both Gwil and Benidic, giving them both a warm smile. "You know you're the best thing that ever happened to my son." His voice was thick with emotion and my heart swelled at the acceptance and pride on his face.

Emotional, I strolled around the counter slinging my arms around both men and tugging them into the sides of my body where they fitted perfectly. Their magic seeped into my soul and made it sing. Duel looks of adoration and love were offered up and I again thanked my lucky stars that Tristan had seen me and decided to interfere in my life.

I gazed back at my father. "They are. They're the magic that was missing from my life."

Groans and laughter filled the shop as I cuffed both men around the ears. "Get back to work, the pair of you. This shoemaker can't have his Elves slacking now, can he?"

They gave me saucy winks as they strolled back through the shop, my father stepping up to my side.

"Nice pun. The Elves and the Shoemaker." He chuckled and shook his head. "That was your favourite story as a young un." He slapped my back and my mouth hung open for a few seconds before I started to laugh.

Who said folk tales couldn't come true!

• • •

The End

Hi all,

Let me introduce myself, I'm JP or Jayne. I'm a lady of a certain age (cough, cough over 50 but I embrace my inner child often). I'm an identical twin and I was born in the Isle of Man; this makes me Manx (not British or English). I've lived in several places over the years but I returned to the island 1998. I love the sea and now it's only a stone's throw from my home.

I quit my nursing career this year to follow my dream to write full time. I published my first book in 2018 and since then I've managed to publish a further twenty plus books. (I have a 12 book challenge this year, and I'm two and a half books away from completing it!)

My island is steeped in folklore and I have used some of this in my writing, particularly the Manx Cat Guardian Series, it's paranormal with a twist. But I'm an eclectic girl and I've spread my wings a little. The tropes vary, Daddy Kink, BDSM, age gap, Billionaire romance, Small town friendships, friends to lovers, out for you, sweet romance, they all have a little angst (or a lot). I tend to write in series and The Elves and the Bondage Daddy lends itself to that too, (shakes head).

Writing has unleashed a beast in my mind and now I can't switch it off. So with that, I now have to try and keep my unruly boys in check while they vie for my attention, and currently it's who shouts the loudest. But, I'm okay with that now I have the time to let the words follow

I hope you have enjoyed this book, and if you are in need of more, then you can find all my other books, on Amazon and in KU.

If you're interested in keeping up to date with what I'm planning then why don't you follow and join me on the following links.

You can find me and follow me on:
Newsletter Sign up
Goodreads
Tumblr
Bookbub
Instagram
Twitter
Facebook
Website address
Facebook Author page
JP Manx Minx's
Patreon

If you would like to give me any feedback or just have any questions, go ahead and friend me on Facebook, and I would be happy to answer anything. Well, almost anything. I hope you enjoyed this book. If you would also like to leave a review, then I would love to read your thoughts.

Thank you for taking the time to be part of my dream.

ALSO BY JP SAYLE

<u>**Standalone**</u>

<u>***When Fake Changed Everything***</u>

<u>**Series**</u>

Potters Creek

<u>***A Christmas Wish (Book One)***</u>

The App Series

<u>***The App: Daddy Kink (book one)***</u>

The App: Littles (book two)

Flamingo Bar

Always More (The Flamingo Bar Book 1)

La Trattoria Di Amore Series

Puzzle Pieces (Book One)

Dominated but not Subdued (Book Two)

The Playroom Series

<u>Mine, Body and Soul: Part One</u>

<u>Mine, Body and Soul: Part Two</u>

__Mine, Body and Soul: Part Three__

__Mine, Body and Soul Trilogy__

Ferron's Journey, Part One: Damaged, The Playroom Series (book four)

Ferron's Journey: Part Two Hidden

Release July 17th 2020

The Manx Cat Guardians Series

Boxset

Where it all Began: Origins (Book 1)

Seeing Beyond the Scars (Book 2)

Destiny Collides Past and Present (Book 3)

Searching for a Soul to Love (Book 4)

The 12 Disasters of Christmas (Book 5)

Laws of Attraction (Book 6)

The Teacher's Boy (Book 7)

Audio Books

Mine, Body and Soul, Part One: The Playroom Series

Narrator Matt Haynes

Mine, Body and Soul, Part Two: The Playroom Series

Narrator Matt Haynes

<u>*Mine, Body and Soul, Part Three: The Playroom Series*</u>

Narrator Matt Haynes

<u>*The App (Daddy Kink) – Book one*</u>

Narrator Matt Haynes

<u>*Always More (The Flamingo Bar Book 1)*</u>

Narrator Matt Haynes

When Fake Changed Everything

Narrator Matt Haynes